"You're not the only one sacrificing.

"Contrary to what you believe, this isn't all about you."

"Prove it," he said, throwing down the gauntlet at her booted feet. When she didn't answer, his lips curved into a mocking, cynical twist. "So much for your pretty speech. Righteous indignation doesn't become you, sweetheart."

"Cain, listen. I—"

"No," he interrupted. Unbidden and without his conscious permission, his gaze raked down her body again. His blood pounded in his veins and he detested that his body could betray him. Could make him weak for her. "You listen. You'll be the one to pay the price. Consider that, Devon. And decide if it's worth it. I promise you. It isn't."

He pivoted and strode from the room, unable to spend another moment staring into those bottomless eyes that had awakened a connection he didn't want to feel.

* * *

Vows in Name Only by Naima Simone is part of the Billionaires of Boston series.

Dear Reader,

Starting a new series is always exciting and also kind of scary. It's the first book that introduces a new world and characters who you really hope— and pray!—the reader falls in love with. But it's also exciting because of the same reasons. New heroes, heroines and families. New stories and intrigue. New drama and, of course, happily-ever-afters. And I hope you, the reader, fall for the gorgeous and complicated Farrell brothers, their wonderful heroines and their glamorous world that is full of secrets.

In *Vows in Name Only*, Cain Farrell discovers that not only does he have two brothers whom he never knew existed, but that in order for him to inherit the family company, they must all work together for a year. And now he's being blackmailed by one of his father's associates. To protect his mother, he'll need to marry this man's daughter. To save the center she loves, Devon acquiesces to her father's machinations. These two are people who have been hurt in the past by the people they love, and trust doesn't come easily to either of them. But an undeniable passion stirs between them, and it might be the very thing that saves them...or could ruin them.

I hope you enjoy this beginning to the Billionaires of Boston series!

Happy reading!

Naima

NAIMA SIMONE

VOWS IN NAME ONLY

HARLEQUIN®
DESIRE™

ISBN-13: 978-1-335-20946-7

Recycling programs
for this product may
not exist in your area.

Vows in Name Only

Copyright © 2020 by Naima Simone

This edition published by arrangement with Harlequin Books S.A.

For questions and comments about the quality of this book,
please contact us at CustomerService@Harlequin.com.

Harlequin Enterprises ULC
22 Adelaide St. West, 40th Floor
Toronto, Ontario M5H 4E3, Canada
www.Harlequin.com

Printed in U.S.A.

USA TODAY bestselling author **Naima Simone**'s love of romance was first stirred by Harlequin books pilfered from her grandmother. Now she spends her days writing sizzling romances with a touch of humor and snark.

She is wife to her own real-life superhero and mother to two awesome kids. They live in perfect domestically challenged bliss in the southern United States.

Books by Naima Simone

Harlequin Desire

Billionaires of Boston

Vows in Name Only

Blackout Billionaires

The Billionaire's Bargain
Black Tie Billionaire
Blame It on the Billionaire

Dynasties: Seven Sins

Ruthless Pride

Visit her Author Profile page at Harlequin.com, or naimasimone.com, for more titles.

You can also find Naima Simone on Facebook, along with other Harlequin Desire authors, at Facebook.com/harlequindesireauthors!

To Gary. 143.

One

"What the hell are you talking about?" Cain Farrell snarled, surging from his chair in his father's library.

His dead father's library.

Barron Farrell had to be dead for Cain to step foot in the mausoleum where he'd suffered a hellish childhood. As soon as he'd graduated from college at twenty-one, he'd left and never returned for a birthday, a Christmas, an Easter or even a potluck dinner. It was bad enough he'd spent twelve-hour workdays with his father at the offices of Farrell International, the conglomerate that had been in his family for four generations. But he'd vowed eleven years ago to never again grace the hallowed halls and marble floors of his father's historic Beacon Hill mansion.

It figured the old man would do something as contrary as having a heart attack and dying just to get Cain to break his promise.

He'd always been a manipulative bastard.

Speaking of bastards…

Cain stalked across the gleaming hardwood floor, ignoring the dark leather furniture gathered around a cavernous fireplace, the winding staircase leading to the next level, the floor-to-cathedral ceiling shelves packed with first editions of the classics his father had never bothered to read. If Cain looked too long, the memories always lurking at the edges of his mind would seize the opportunity to slither in and torment him. To inflict punishments like the ones he'd received in front of the very desk behind which Daryl Holleran, his father's personal attorney, perched.

God, Cain hated this room. This whole goddamn house.

Fury bristled inside him. He drew to a halt in front of a large bay window, but the view of the private walled garden didn't consume his attention. No, the other two men sitting silently in the room claimed that distinction.

Two strangers he'd never laid eyes on before this afternoon. Two strangers whose presence had been requested at the reading of Barron's will.

Two strangers who, according to Daryl, were Cain's brothers.

Half brothers.

"Cain," Daryl said, his smooth baritone placating, as if he hadn't just announced that the multibillion-dollar company Cain had been groomed to run was no longer his. "I know this is surprising—"

Cain snorted, pivoting and jabbing his tightly balled fists into the pockets of his black suit pants. "Surprising? No, surprising is Big Papi coming out of retirement and returning to the Sox. Surprising is finally discovering the location of Jimmy Hoffa's body. Surprising is the Four Horsemen of the Apocalypse riding down Commonwealth. This, Daryl, is bullshit," he snapped.

To his credit, the older man didn't flinch at Cain's caustic tone. But then again, Daryl had been Barron Farrell's lawyer for the past thirty years. The man probably had skin as thick as an elephant's ass.

"Be that as it may," Daryl said, picking up the small stack of papers from the desk, "it was your father's decision, and Barron was adamant and very clear about the terms. Controlling shares in Farrell International are to go to his living heirs. But only if you and your brothers agree to remain in Boston and run the company together for the period of a year, starting from the date this will is read. At the end of the year, you can decide to helm it together, or Cain, you can buy out your brothers' shares and Farrell International is yours. If any of you refuse to adhere to these conditions, then the company and all its subsidiaries will be liquidated and sold to the highest bidders."

It didn't make any more sense the second time around.

"There's one more stipulation," Daryl added.

"Of course there is," Cain growled.

"It concerns you, Cain." Daryl paused, and for the first time, Cain glimpsed uneasiness flash in the older man's brown eyes. Which set off an almost painful tightening of his stomach. If this unflappable man was discomfited, that spelled trouble for Cain. "You must spend the next year here. In this house."

Cain didn't move—couldn't. Because if he even dragged in a breath, he would explode, and the fury that howled inside him would consume this room and the people in it. Barron hadn't been satisfied with hijacking Cain's future. No, he had to manipulate his son into his own personal nightmare.

That son of a *bitch*.

"So just because the asshole who knocked up my mother demands it, I'm supposed to give up my life in Washington and move here?" The bearded giant in the black thermal shirt, faded jeans and battered brown boots who Daryl had called Achilles shook his head. "She might have given me his last name, but that's all I got from him. I don't owe him a damn thing."

Or you.

Achilles didn't say the words aloud, but they quivered in the air, and Cain ground his teeth together. Of course, the possible dismantlement of the business Cain had worked on for most of his life wouldn't affect this man. Losing the business for which he had endured the intolerant, merciless Barron, the business Cain had dreamed of one day heading…that wouldn't concern this man either.

He hadn't suffered for it.

Hadn't sacrificed for it.

But Cain had.

It was his legacy. His due for surviving and outliving Barron Farrell.

And yet, Barron had found a way to rip it all out from under him.

"I have to admit, when I received the phone call to attend this mysterious gathering, I wasn't expecting a family reunion," the second man, Kenan Rhodes, drawled, eyebrows arched over the distinctive blue-gray eyes they all shared. Farrell eyes. "But I have to agree with Achilles, is it?" At the giant's nod, Kenan shrugged a suit jacket–covered shoulder. "I have a position with my family's business. A good one. And leaving it would be like turning my back on them. What would be my incentive to do that? I didn't know Barron Farrell personally, but I am aware of his reputation. And no offense, but I have no reason to give him my loyalty."

Cain stared at the two strangers, and though the will had announced them as brothers, he felt no pull toward them. No familial connection. Hell, except for the eyes, none of them would be mistaken for family.

Kenan, with his light brown skin, close-cropped dark hair and neat goatee, was biracial. Though they all shared tall, muscular frames, Cain and Kenan were wide-shouldered and lean, while Achilles boasted a broad, powerful build that wouldn't be out of place on a football defensive line. Add in the shoulder-length, nearly black, curly hair, beard and tawny skin and he rounded out the most diverse family tree since Brad and Angelina's children.

Still… That Cain's father had cheated on his mother didn't shock him. His infidelity hadn't been a secret in their house. What astonished him was that Barron had fathered not one, but two illegitimate children. Barron might not have cared where he stuck his dick but the thought that he would leave the fate of his company to the whims of men he hadn't known? Cain couldn't line that up with the controlling bastard his father had been.

But then, apparently Barron had been aware of his sons all the time. And he hadn't bothered to acknowledge their existence until it benefited him. Until he could shift and maneuver all three of them like pawns on a chessboard.

Now *that* coincided with the Barron Farrell Cain knew.

"I don't expect your loyalty, and I'm not asking for it," Cain stated. His flat tone belied the anger and yes, fear, roiling in his veins. "Both of you are right—you have your lives. But today, mine just changed forever. Not only did I find out I have two brothers I never knew existed, but everything I've—" *suffered for* "—worked for is suddenly not in my control but in the hands of strangers who, as you put it, don't owe me a damn thing. Yes, you can walk away, and nothing changes for you. For me, though? *Everything changes.* I don't have the option of walking away."

Panic welled up in him. "I don't have—"

A legacy. Control. Power. A voice.

His teeth snapped shut, grinding together, trapping those betraying words inside him. Trapping the plea that would inevitably follow.

Had his father resented him this much—hated him this much—that even from the grave he relished the thought of Cain humiliating himself to beg these strangers to help him? To save him?

Yes. Yes, he had.

The swift and concise answer rebounded against Cain's skull and everything he'd ever felt for his father—rage, grief, confusion, bitterness and God help him, love—swirled in his chest like a tornado.

"Fuck this," he growled, stalking across the room and wrenching the heavy library door open to storm out. Air. He needed air that wasn't tainted by his desperation and helplessness. By his weakness.

Almost immediately the incongruous sounds of gaiety slapped him as he stepped into the hallway. Right. The reception. How screwed up was it that the circus in the library had temporarily made him forget that over a hundred people congregated in the great room and formal dining room to mourn his father? He snorted. Mourn, hell. From the loud chatter, bright laughter and clink of glassware, he couldn't tell if they were all there to celebrate his life—or his death.

Exhaling, Cain pivoted sharply and strode toward the rear of the house, in the opposite direction of his "guests." In his current mood, he wasn't good company and he damn sure didn't feel like fielding condolences.

At least Barron was in a better place.

If one could call hell a better place.

Two

Devon Cole frowned at the wall of shrubbery in front of her, two thoughts prevalent in her mind.

One, how in the world did the gardener manage to keep the leaves so green and lush in the middle of October? A special fertilizer? A new pesticide? The blood of virgins?

And two, if she waited a few seconds longer, would David Bowie dressed as the Goblin King appear wearing his eyebrow-raising buff breeches and Tina Turner hair?

They were both fair questions considering she stood outside in a garden with high, labyrinthine hedges that formed cozy nooks and convenient, romantic hiding places. Who would've thought such a beautiful, magical place could exist behind a cold mausoleum of a mansion? Unless this was where the owner banished those who displeased him to be devoured by a voracious minotaur?

Oh, and a third thought… She peered down into the flute of red wine she clasped in her hand. Should this third glass of cabernet sauvignon be her last? When a person started wondering about garden tips, David Bowie's codpiece and Greek mythology in the space of ten seconds, laying off the booze might be wise.

Sighing, she stared down into her glass. She'd only briefly met Barron Farrell a few times at the social events her father had browbeaten her into attending, but still… The dead deserved respect. If not for Barron, then at least for the son he'd left behind.

Her belly clenched as an image of Cain Farrell coalesced in her mind. She'd never encountered Barron Farrell's son and heir before today; not surprising since she tried to avoid the galas, charity events and dinner parties her father so loved.

Closing her eyes, she sank to one of the marble benches dotting the cool, shadowed corners of the garden. She'd attended the crowded, solemn funeral at the ornate Catholic church, but only at the graveside ceremony had she captured her first view of Cain Farrell. Even from several rows back, it hadn't been hard to spot him. Not when he towered above most of the people there.

Even unsmiling and stoic, he'd been…beautiful. A lean, angular face with slashing cheekbones, almost brutally perfect lines, a carnal yet hard mouth and a stark, uncompromising jaw. His black, slim-fitting, ruthlessly tailored suit had molded to wide shoulders, broad chest, slim waist and long, muscular legs. A king. He reminded her of a king who bore authority as his birthright, but who'd have no issue with throwing on armor and hefting a sword and shield to fight beside his men. Commanding, formidable, and merciless when warranted. Matter of fact, the only thing soft about him had been the thick, dark waves combed back from his face and curling around his ears and the collar of his jacket. Yet, instead of gentling his imposing, arrogant beauty, those incongruously soft strands only emphasized the blunt, raw strength of his facial features, especially the hint of cruelty in the sensual curves of his mouth...

Shame threaded through her.

He'd been mourning his father, and she'd been ogling him as if he'd been Mr. December in a Billionaires of the Year calendar. Maybe her father was right, and he really *couldn't* take her anywhere.

A piercing longing stabbed her in the chest, and she pressed a palm over her heart, rubbing the phantom soreness. Ten years she'd been in this world of wealth, and she still didn't fit in. No amount of etiquette classes or designer wardrobes could remedy that.

What she wouldn't give to be gone from this Beacon Hill home, hell, from *Boston*, and be back in their old house in Plainfield, New Jersey, that had been full of family, with her and her parents on one side of the duplex, and her uncle, aunt and three cousins on the other. Their home had been crowded, relatives flowing from one apartment to the other with slamming doors, loud voices and laughter. Their home had been happy.

That had been before her mother had died from a lingering cough that she'd refused to see the doctor about. A cough that had evolved into a severe case of pneumonia. That had been before her father had channeled his grief, anger and ambition into growing his chain of electronics stores, eventually selling to a larger company. That had been before he'd invested profit from the sale in a tech company that would lead the industry in defense-level security and go from respectably wealthy to filthy rich.

That had been before he decided Plainfield was too "boorish" for him and his daughter—his words, not hers. She loved her hometown, loved her family. But he'd cut off all ties and moved them to Boston where his job had become infiltrating the rarified ranks of the blue bloods of high society. Ranks into which all his nouveau riche money couldn't buy entrance.

Didn't stop him from trying though.

Hence, their presence at Barron Farrell's funeral. Her father hadn't been able to pass up an opportunity to rub elbows in this affluent circle of businessmen, socialites and celebrities. But to be fair, he wasn't the only one treating the billionaire's death like a tea party.

Heaving another sigh, she picked up her glass and rose from the bench. She'd better head back inside before her father came looking for her with his constantly disappointed and disapproving scowl. Her fingers tightened around the stem, and she briefly closed her eyes, weathering the momentary vise on her heart. God, she remembered a time when only affection, love and pride had brightened his dark eyes. That had been when he'd been a husband and father, content with a couple of stores. That'd been before death had cleaved their lives in two.

Staring at the pointed toes of her black Louis Vuittons, she stepped back on the paved garden path, dragging.

"Damn you."

The low, rumbling growl reached her seconds before a tall, powerful figure stalked around the row of hedges, pausing inches away from her. The corner of the shrubbery offered her flimsy cover, and she clung to it, gaping at the man pacing back and forth. From the bench she'd just vacated to the wall across the slim path and back again.

Not just a man.

Cain Farrell.

Anger seemed to vibrate off his large frame in humid waves. No, not anger. *Fury.* With his black hair, black suit and dangerous stride, he resembled a predator. Sleek, dark and lethal. Waiting for the right prey to cross his path so he could pounce…devour.

Did it make her foolish that she couldn't ascertain if she wanted to avoid becoming said prey, or…or surrender to the insane need to soothe him? To pet his hair, stroke those broad shoulders? Yes, it did make her a fool. Because one did *not* try and comfort a beast on the hunt.

Even if he was an incredibly sexy beast…

Cain jerked to a halt, pinning her with a narrowed but brilliant stare and jamming her breath in her lungs.

Damn.

"Who are you?" he demanded. His voice was constructed of midnight, the most expensive Scotch…and dark chocolate. Yummy.

"Me?" she rasped. Oh God. She mentally shook her head, but then made the mistake of looking into the absolute beauty of his eyes. Wow. Given the distance between them, she hadn't determined the color at the cemetery. But now… "I'd wondered," she breathed.

Dark, arrogant brows slanted down over his startling, blue-gray eyes. A wolf's eyes. The sense of being in the presence of a predator grew, but instead of fear, excitement tinged with nerves hummed under her skin.

Don't be silly.

"You wondered what?" Cain asked, impatience a tight snap in his voice.

"Your eyes," she blurted out, inwardly wincing and cursing her decision to pick up that third glass of wine. Shrugging a shoulder, she added, "I couldn't tell the color at the graveside service. But now, I, uh, know," she finished. Lamely. Scrounging for a smile, she moved forward, erasing the scant distance separating them. "Devon."

She stretched her hand toward him—the hand not clutching the wineglass for dear life. For several taut seconds, he glared down at it, then slowly lifted his arm.

His long, elegant fingers engulfed hers. Branding her. Fire licked at her palm, blazed up her arm and swirled in her chest like a star seconds from imploding. His gaze rose from their clasped hands and traveled the path the flames had taken. Only his gaze dipped lower, taking in the rest of her petite frame before finally landing on her face again.

Extricating her hand from his, she fought the need to rub her tingling palm against her thigh. She hiked up her chin to meet his wolf's gaze. She knew what he saw. What everyone saw. Short. Nondescript features. She'd overheard one "gentleman" call her forgettable. Breasts and hips too heavy and rounded to be fashionable. Her best feature was the thick, caramel curls that were wrapped in a knot at the back of her head now, but when loose, reached the middle of her back. Her mother's hair.

No, she wasn't a great beauty, and no doubt he dated women whose faces belonged on big screens and whose bodies graced swimwear magazines, but screw it. One of her first lessons after moving to Boston had been never, *ever* let anyone know they could intimidate her. The first whiff of weakness and they circled like vultures over a carcass. Being on the receiving end of that attack one too many times, her motto was now, *Fake it until you get home and barricade yourself in your bedroom with chips, ranch dip and Netflix.*

It worked for her.

Cain stared at her, silent and brooding. And even though she shook inside, she didn't waver. But, damn, those eyes. Eerie in their beauty. Like he could see past flesh and bone, down to her soul…

"Yes, now you know," he drawled, and the flames that had died down to a simmer burst to life…in her face. *Oh God.* He probably thought that was her pathetic attempt at flirting. "What are you doing out here,

Devon?" he asked. "The *party*," his lips curled into a faint sneer, "is in the house. Specifically, the great and dining rooms. This part of the property is off-limits to guests."

"Oh, I'm sorry. I must've missed the signs," she apologized. As soon as the words echoed between them, it hit her how flippant they sounded. "I mean, of course there weren't *signs*. But in a house this size, maybe there should be. Or at least little discreet nameplates like on bathroom doors—*oh dammit*."

"Excuse me?" Cain growled, his frown deepening.

She shook her head, holding up a finger in the universal sign of "Wait a minute." And she took that minute to take a deep gulp of wine. And another. "Honest to God, I'm more of a sipper and two glasses is my limit. I don't know what made me think I could handle three. Here." She thrust the goblet at him, and he accepted it. Either that or wear it. "Besides, given you were just damning someone minutes ago, you probably could use it more than me."

Again, more staring on his part. And could she really blame him? She was acting like a lunatic. A tipsy, blathering, garden-invading lunatic.

Slowly, without breaking his visual connection to her, he lifted the glass to his beautiful, cruel mouth. And sipped.

Her knees might not have weakened, but by God, they wobbled. Why that sip was so hot, she couldn't begin to explain. But the heat gathering low in her belly and flowing to all points north and south assured her, it most definitely was.

"You're right," he said. "I need it. Thank you."

The wine. He needed the wine. Not *her*, as her body wanted to interpret his words.

"You're welcome." Unable to maintain peering into his unusual gaze, she brushed invisible lint from the skirt of her dark gray sheath dress. And as she recovered the space she'd placed between them, all embarrassment and disconcerting desire fled. "God, I was so focused on heading back to hell, I forgot." She reached out to him, placing a hand on his forearm. Taut muscle flexed beneath her fingers and his jacket. But she didn't allow it to distract her. "I'm so sorry for the loss of your father. Unfortunately, I know the pain you're feeling, and I wouldn't wish it on anyone."

His scrutiny dropped to his arm, where her fingers still lingered. He didn't move out from under her touch, and though it would've been the smarter option, she didn't remove her hand.

"Heading back to hell?" he repeated, not acknowledging her condolences. She got it; after her mother died, she'd wanted to talk about anything other than her death. "Other than the obvious, where is that?"

She winced, her shoulders lifting to her ears. "Promise not to be offended?" He arched a dark eyebrow but nodded. "That reception. Large social events are my definition of cruel and unusual punishment, but that in there…" She shook her head. "I'm from a big, loud Italian family, so I'm not a stranger to repasts that turn into noisy gatherings with food and laughter. But not like that. There's no one talking about your father, remembering him. There's no sense of sadness that comes with losing someone you love. There aren't any tears with the laughter. There's no comfort from family and friends. What I escaped in there is…ghoulish."

She lowered her hand from his arm and braced herself for his rebuke. Prepared herself for the same chiding smirk she'd received from her father when she'd voiced the same thoughts before seeking a place where she could get a break from the avarice and phoniness of it all.

But the ridicule didn't come.

Instead, Cain studied her with an impenetrable stare that revealed nothing. That must be a handy skill.

She fought not to fidget under his regard, but just as she parted her lips to apologize for her insensitive words, he murmured, "Thank you, Devon."

"For?" Being inappropriately blunt? Trespassing? Handing him secondhand wine? He had to be more specific.

"For having the courage to be honest when the truth isn't pretty." A small, half smile that struck her as a shade grim briefly curved a corner of his sensual mouth. "And for giving me a few minutes' reprieve from my own hell." He stretched the glass of wine back toward her, and as she accepted it, he lifted his other hand and shocked her by stroking the back of his fingers down her cheek. "I appreciate that more than you know."

He stepped away, leaving her skin burning from his caress. She didn't move —couldn't move— as he sharply pivoted on his heel and strode away, disappearing as quickly and quietly as he'd appeared.

Only then did she graze her trembling fingers over the spot he'd touched so tenderly. With gratitude. Because surely, she'd imagined the flash of heat in his eyes. It'd been only a wishful reflection of the unwise and wistful desire that had coursed through her.

Yes, that's all.

Still, what was the harm in believing in that fantasy?

It wasn't like she would see Cain Farrell again.

Nope. No harm at all.

Three

A year.

That was the length of time required of him, and he could endure it. Hell, he'd endured his father for thirty-two years. Twelve more months was child's play.

He could damn well do this.

The mantra marched through Cain's head like a regiment of soldiers on a deadly campaign, and he clenched his jaw so tightly it throbbed. Either that or let loose the string of curses flaying his throat. And he would never give his father that satisfaction. Dead or alive.

"Mr. Farrell, you had several messages while you were in your meeting. I placed them on your desk and emailed them to you as well," Charlene Gregg, his executive assistant, informed him as he stalked past her desk. The polished brunette had been with him for the last five years, and she was a godsend. Her protective, six-foot-four, three-hundred-pound bruiser of a husband and adorable two children thought so as well.

"Thanks, Charlene," he ground out. Another perk of having an assistant who'd been with him so long. She ignored his bad moods. "Hold all calls for the next twenty minutes."

"Of course."

He entered his office, barely managing not to slam the door behind him. Control. He'd spent the formative years of his childhood developing it. Growing up in a chaotic household where the slightest offense—real or imagined—could earn him a verbal, soul-stripping assault or a punch to the chest, he'd been a quick study on reining in his emotions and reactions.

But coming out of a meeting with his... Hell, he still couldn't call them his brothers. Achilles Farrell, the brooding giant who shared his last name, and Kenan Rhodes, the charmer with the wide smile and steely eyes, were strangers. Strangers who, only a week after their initial meeting during the funeral reception, were carving a piece out of his company for their own.

He hated the intrusion.

Guilt thrummed inside his chest, but the simmering anger that had become his constant companion prevented it from sinking a foothold. Logically, he got that his rage was directed toward a dead man who'd screwed him over, but Barron wasn't here. His illegitimate offspring were.

Thrusting a hand through his hair, Cain circled his desk and dropped into his chair. His gaze lit on the thick file he'd been studying for the past week. Immediately after the will reading, Cain had contacted Farrell International's private detective and had him open investigations on Achilles and Kenan.

Achilles Farrell. Born in Boston, but raised by a single mother near Seattle, Washington. Software developer and something of a genius. And an ex-con who'd spent two years in jail for assault. Seemed like a chip off the old block.

Kenan Rhodes. Born and raised in Boston by the wealthy family who'd adopted him. VP of Marketing in his family's business and brilliant at it. And a consummate ladies' man, according to the number of times he appeared in society gossip pages. Again, chip off the old block.

And once both men had agreed to Barron's terms, they'd informed Cain they didn't plan on sitting back as figureheads while the year crawled by. Each intended to make their mark on the company. Achilles with the IT department and Kenan in Marketing. Everything in Cain howled at handing over the reins of any part of his business to strangers. But, because of Barron's will, Cain couldn't object. Couldn't do anything but sit there, fuming. And powerless. That grated the most. As soon as he left his father's house, he'd vowed never to be weak, vulnerable again. And yet...

He raised his arm, his fingers curled into a fist, and aimed it toward his desktop. But at the last moment, he halted the swift downward motion before his hand could slam onto the wood.

Control. He couldn't lose it.

Heaving a sigh, he leaned back, squeezing his eyes closed and pinching the bridge of his nose. Unbidden and inexplicable, an image of Devon—he never did ask her last name—wavered then solidified across the screen of his mind.

It wasn't the first time the woman who'd appeared in his mother's garden like a pinup version of a fairy featured in his thoughts. Petite, with breasts he suspected would spill into his palms. A cinched-in waist that those same hands could easily span. A delicious flare of hips that completed a wicked hourglass figure. The stilettos she'd worn should've added height to her small frame, but they hadn't. Yet, damn had they done amazing things for her toned, thick thighs.

Yes, Devon possessed a body that made a man jerk awake in the middle of the night, sweating, his dick strangled in his fist. But her body couldn't compare to the beautiful emerald eyes that seemed so innocent yet contained age-old secrets in their depths. Or to the gentle slope of her elegant cheekbones that he hadn't been able to resist touching. Or the lush, damn near indecent curve of her mouth that even now had a dull ache throbbing in his hardening flesh. That top lip–heavy mouth had combatted the impression of purity that stubbornly clung to her.

What man could look at her and not lust to be the one who thoroughly corrupted her?

He wasn't that man.

Objectively, he acknowledged that some men might call her features plain or unremarkable.

And those men would be fucking blind.

Yet… Out of all that, it was the humor, the self-deprecation, the sympathy and selfless comfort she offered in her guileless words and wine that calmed him. A week ago, she'd unknowingly given him the strength to return to that library and face his father's mess.

Cain, who lauded himself on needing no one, clung to the memory of a woman he'd met once and would most likely not see again. The irony was not lost on him.

"Mr. Farrell." Charlene's voice through his phone's intercom ripped him from his thoughts and he jerked forward with a grimace. "I know you instructed me not to interrupt you, but there is a Gregory Cole here requesting to see you. He doesn't have an appointment, but he claims it has something personal to do with your father."

Tension streaked through him, and for a moment a terse "no" burned his tongue. Who just showed up uninvited at the executive offices of a billion-dollar company asking for an unscheduled meeting with the CEO? It could be one of the many journalists he'd turned away with a barely polite "No comment." Hell, it could be another brother.

He jabbed the reply button, irritation swirling in his gut. No, whoever it was could turn around and walk out the way they came in. And if it was that important, he could set an appointment before he left.

"Send him in, Charlene." Releasing the button, he rose behind his desk, growling, "Dammit."

His father. And personal. He wanted to resist the lure of that bait, but couldn't.

Moments later, Charlene entered his office, an older

man following close behind her. Tall and distinguished with neatly cut salt-and-pepper hair and clothed in a perfectly tailored suit Cain knew cost at least three thousand dollars, he strode forward, hand outstretched.

"Mr. Farrell, Gregory Cole," he greeted. "I'm glad to meet you, although I wish it were under different circumstances. I was very sorry to hear about your father's passing."

The words were appropriate but his gaze, green and somehow familiar, didn't hold the solemnity that matched. Disquiet crawled beneath Cain's skin as he quickly shook the man's hand and dropped it.

"Thank you, Mr. Cole." He nodded at Charlene who quietly closed the office door behind her. "My assistant said this had to do with my father," he said, sliding his hands into the front pockets of his pants.

No, he didn't invite Gregory Cole to sit down in one of the visitors chairs or on the dark brown leather couch in his sitting area. Call it intuition or plain old superstition, something about the man unnerved him.

"Please, call me Gregory. May I?" He didn't wait for Cain's agreement, but settled into the wingback chair in front of the desk. Crossing one leg over the other, the older man smiled. And superstitious or not, Cain couldn't suppress the shudder that rippled down his spine. "I have a matter regarding my…relationship with your father but decided to wait in deference to your mourning before approaching you."

A whole week. Yes, he was a saint. But given most journalists had been camped out on Cain's doorstep the night of Barron's death, maybe Gregory had been magnanimous.

"Did you have a business relationship with him, Mr. Cole?" Cain questioned, deliberately using the man's surname.

If the slight irritated Gregory, he didn't reveal it. If anything, his smile deepened slightly, and a gleam brightened his gaze.

"I would call it more of an understanding," he drawled, brushing an imaginary speck of lint off his immaculate suit. The gesture was contrived. Deliberate. And annoying. Impatience hummed inside Cain even as Gregory continued, "Mr. Farrell, or Cain. Can I call you Cain?"

"No."

This time the other man couldn't control the brief tightening around his mouth or the flash of anger in his eyes. The telltale signs were there and gone in seconds, but Cain caught them. From the way this man had strolled into his offices with a sense of entitlement, he obviously didn't like hearing the word *no*. Too fucking bad.

"As I was saying… I am a self-made man. I grew a chain of successful electronics stores on my own before selling them and investing the profit in even more lucrative projects. Now I own an exclusive financial and investment firm that has earned my clients and myself millions for the last few years," he bragged.

"Your hard work and determination are very admirable. But I fail to see what that has to do with me or my father. Mr. Cole, I don't want to appear rude and rush you, but I have meetings, so if we could conclude this one…?"

Actually, he didn't give a damn about appearing rude or rushing him.

Again, he caught a glimmer of irritation before something else replaced it. Satisfaction.

Cain's stomach tightened, and though it defied explanation, he braced himself. Because something was coming. And whatever put that gloating shine in Gregory Cole's eyes couldn't mean anything good for Cain.

"By all means," Gregory purred, linking his fingers across his torso. "Before your father died, he entered into a contractual agreement with me. Now that he's gone, it's your responsibility to honor it."

Cain frowned. "That's what we have a legal department for," he said. "If you want to leave the contract with my assistant, she'll make sure it's forwarded to the correct channels—"

"I can do that, *Cain*," he continued, emphasizing the usage of Cain's first name with no small amount of delight. "I thought you might want to keep this particular piece of business private. But if you don't mind your company's attorneys reviewing a wedding contract, I don't either."

Cain blinked. Stared at the man wearing the mocking grin. Shock buffeted him, momentarily rendering him deaf except for two blaring words—*wedding contract*.

What the *fuck*?

That sense of unease exploded into panic and a strangling sensation of claustrophobia. His fingers curled inside his pocket. But ingrained, brutally taught lessons kept him still. Maintained his stoic composure. Betrayed nothing of the fear ricocheting against his rib cage.

Revealed nothing of the weakness.

"What are you talking about?" he asked, voice calm.

"I'm talking about you, Cain Farrell, marrying my daughter. Your father promised you to me. Signed you over to me, actually."

Gregory chuckled as if the thought of a father selling his son like medieval chattel amused him. Hell, since the bastard was doing the same to his own daughter, he probably did find it funny. He opened his jacket and reached inside, withdrawing folded up sheets of paper. Rising, he extended them toward Cain. "I took the precaution of bringing a copy of the contract with me. Please take your time and review it. I assure you it's all binding."

Numb, Cain retrieved the papers and circled his desk. Unfolding the contract, he laid it out and studied it. Silence ticked by in thunderous pulses, echoing the pounding in his veins. And the longer he read, the more consuming his fury became. As he flipped to the last page of the three-page agreement and spied his father's bold scrawl next to Gregory's more elegant signature, Cain's body ached with the force he wielded to restrain himself. To not roar his outrage to the ceiling. To not flip his fucking desk. To not lunge across the space separating him from the smirking bastard across from him and wrap his hands around his scheming neck.

"You call yourself a businessman," Cain ground out,

his voice the consistency of gravel. "You forgot to add a couple more names. Extortionist. Blackmailer."

Gregory didn't even possess the decency to appear ashamed of his actions. Lifting a shoulder in a Gallic shrug, he arched an eyebrow. "No need to get insulting, Cain. One thing I learned during my climb up in this world, no one is going to offer handouts to a poor man with a high school education. I made my own success. Forged my own paths when people of *your world* closed them. And I did that by any means necessary. So if you expect me to apologize or feel ashamed for how I got here, then you're in for a long wait that will only end in disappointment."

"Save me that self-serving drivel," Cain snapped, uncaring if Gregory glared at him in return. "There are plenty of people who start from the bottom, who put in the work, the sacrifice to claw their way to the top without resorting to criminal behavior. So you weren't born with a trust fund. Over ninety percent of people aren't. But you denigrate their efforts and shame them by justifying this—" he jabbed a finger at the offensive contract "—with where you started from."

"Spoken like a man who's never gone a day without in his life," Gregory sneered, a ruddy color flooding his sharp cheekbones. A cold rage glinted in his green eyes, and Cain correctly deciphered the disgust there. For him.

"You don't know a goddamn thing about me, Cole," Cain growled, planting his fists on the desktop and leaning forward. "Because if you did, you would've never walked into my office this morning. Take this."

He flicked the three sheets of paper, and they slid across the furniture, teetering on the edge before fluttering to the floor. "And get the hell out."

Gregory didn't bend to pick up the contract or remove his stare from Cain's.

"Oh see, that's where you're wrong. I know all I need to when it comes to you, Cain," he murmured, a corner of his mouth kicking up in a smirk Cain hungered to knock off his face. "While your father entered into this arrangement because of his conceit and ego, he assured me you would comply because of one thing. Your loyalty to your mother. A love for one's mother—it's a powerful thing," he continued in a silky tone. "And I don't doubt that you would do anything rather than see Emelia Farrell's name splashed across tabloid rags and dragged through the gutter by unscrupulous reporters. They would be relentless if they discovered that she had an affair while still married to your father. And they would be absolutely rabid if they received evidence of that affair—pictures, emails, texts…video."

Bile rushed from his stomach in an acidic torrent. It burned, searing him. For an instant, he caved to the pain and briefly closed his eyes. But immediately, images of his mother's face if this news became public swam across the backs of his lids. Devastated. Humiliated. Broken.

His mother, beautiful, proud, kind and so damn strong. In order to be married to Barron Farrell she'd had to be. She'd been the one stable, loving constant in Cain's life—gentle where his father had been harsh. Affectionate where he'd been cold. Protective when he'd been the aggressor. She'd suffered during her marriage. Once upon a time she'd probably loved his father, but his belittling, verbal assaults and constant infidelities had whittled that devotion to scraps. And his insistence on "making a man" of Cain with his fists had eradicated even those remnants.

His mother had endured for Cain, and the knowledge, the guilt, ate at him. She could've left Barron at any time, but he would've fought her for custody, and with his power, money and influence, Barron would've won. And she'd refused to leave Cain to Barron's "tender mercies." So she'd stayed until Cain had been old enough to fend for himself both financially and physically.

Emelia Farrell had paid her dues.

So no, he didn't blame her for stepping outside her travesty of a marriage and finding comfort where she could. Just... *Christ.* She'd made a mistake choosing this man.

"Another crime you're confessing to, Cole," Cain snarled, loathing scalding him from the inside out. "It's against the law to release that kind of material without the other party's consent."

"Sue me."

Cain straightened. Better to insert as much distance between them as possible. "And your daughter? She doesn't care that the man she's willing to chain herself to is only marrying her because of blackmail? That he doesn't want her, doesn't love her? Or is she like you, and all she cares about is digging her hooks into a wealthy man so she can bleed him dry?"

"My daughter does what needs to be done for her

family," he replied, smoothly. "And I don't need your money, Cain. I have more than enough of that. But if my daughter is married to a Farrell, doors that money can't buy will be opened to her."

"To you, you mean," Cain spat.

Another shrug. "Boston society is clannish, disdainful to those who weren't born in your rarefied circles. You know as well as I do that wealth will only propel a person so far. Will only grant them entrance to the building, but not a seat at the table. If you're born with a setting and a name card at that table, then you can't talk to me about how to gain a place there."

Bitterness tinged the other man's words, and though Cain hated Gregory for his methods, for threatening his mother, Cain had to agree with him on that point.

He understood the cliquish, snobby and classist world he moved in. Understood that more often than not it was the name Farrell and everything it meant—history, heritage, power, affluence—that paved his way, granted him access, afforded him allowances others didn't have.

But nothing, *nothing*, excused Gregory Cole.

He'd threatened the only person Cain cared about. That was unforgivable. Of him and his daughter.

"So when it comes down to it, you and your bitch of a daughter are willing to sell other people's souls for business," Cain said, voice as cold as the sheet of ice spreading through his veins.

"Business. Connections. Power. Influence. Your father understood that better than most," he corrected. The smile curving his mouth disappeared and the humor fled Gregory's eyes. "Enough chitchat. As you mentioned, you have meetings and I have appointments as well. So what is your answer, Cain? Are you going to marry my daughter or am I going to release my information about your mother's dalliance to the media?"

For an instant, Cain transformed into that ten-year-old boy cowering in front of his father in that damn library. Cowering and crying because he wanted to fight back, to break free and be strong enough to face his father down. But he couldn't then. And he couldn't now. Once more he was as powerless and helpless as that boy.

Gregory Cole had made him go back on his vow never to be that weak, that vulnerable again.

And Cole would pay for that.

He and his daughter.

"I agree to marry her," Cain said, meeting the triumph in those green eyes. "But that's all I'm agreeing to. You've consigned your daughter to a union from hell. I'll make sure of it. She'll get my name and nothing more. You might have forged this farce of a marriage, but she's going to be the one to suffer for it. I promise you that."

Four

"Devon, is that you?"

Devon closed the front door behind her, momentarily holding on to the doorknob. *Lord, give me strength*, she silently prayed. And then grimaced, guilt for the disloyal thought scurrying though her. No matter how… *demanding* her father could be, he was still her father. And even if he'd changed so drastically from the protective, affectionate and laughing man he used to be when her mother was alive, he'd still never abandoned her. He'd provided for her, given her everything any daughter could wish for…everything money could buy.

"Yes, Dad, it's me," she called out, setting her purse on a chair then striding through the spacious foyer of the stately brick town house located in the heart of Back Bay.

Her father had shelled out seven million for the

home—and he had zero problems bragging about it to anyone. It was gorgeous; she couldn't deny it. With large, airy rooms and cathedral ceilings, oversized bay windows that offered views of the quiet tree-lined street and the private patio, cavernous fireplaces, beautiful bedrooms and luxurious bathrooms, it was a place Devon couldn't have ever imagined calling home as a little girl. The one-bedroom apartment on the garden level even provided an elegantly appointed home office for her father. Add in the expensive art pieces, opulent furniture and state-of-the-art amenities, it was a showpiece.

And yet, for Gregory Cole, it still didn't seem to be enough. Her father had this yawning, insatiable hole inside him that he tried to fill with money and things. A hole that family used to fill.

Smothering a sigh, she entered the casual living room. Her father stood in front of the dormant fireplace big enough to fit two grown men. Well, maybe one and a half if the men were the size of Cain Farrell—okay, she had to stop thinking about him.

It'd been a little over a week since that impromptu meeting in his garden, and she couldn't eradicate him from her mind. More than was probably healthy, she turned those stolen moments over and over, analyzing them. Trying to convince herself that his gentle stroke to her cheek hadn't meant anything beyond gratitude. That she hadn't spied heat in his eyes. Because to believe the alternative…

"Hey, Dad," she greeted. "Is everything okay? Your message sounded urgent."

"Yes, everything is okay. Better than okay," he said, flicking a hand. A frown creased his forehead as he scanned her from top to bottom. "Good Lord, Devon. What are you wearing? I can't believe you went out looking like that. What if one of my business associates or someone important had seen you?" He shook his head, uttering a low sound of disappointment.

Someone important had seen her. Several *someones* actually. The hundred-plus children she worked with as a youth coordinator at a community center located in East Boston.

"Since most schools are out for Columbus Day, we hosted a play day. Jeans and a shirt are far more appropriate for balloon tosses, three-legged races and kickball than a suit." Very aware of her father's low opinion of her job—a job he viewed as beneath her—she shoved aside the pang of hurt his condescending words elicited and switched the subject. "So what's going on? Why did I need to rush home?"

Before replying, he crossed the room to the full bar built into the wall. Only after he fixed himself a drink and sipped from it did he turn back to her. "I have wonderful news, Devon," he said, lightly swirling the alcohol in his glass. "We're having a very special guest over for dinner. Which means you need to go upstairs, get out of those rags and dress in your best."

"That's the emergency?" She left off the *seriously*. But it echoed in the room. "You have people over for dinner at least three times a week. Why is this so important?"

"Because," he paused, sipping from the glass and

studying her over the rim, "the guest is your future husband."

Devon rocked back on the heels of her sneakers in shock. The words boomed in her head, but they didn't make sense. Husband? What the hell was he talking about? She wasn't even *seeing* someone much less thinking about marriage.

Swallowing hard past a suddenly constricted throat, she forced out, "What?"

"I've arranged for you to be married to one of the most sought-after bachelors in this city. Maybe the country. He comes from one of Boston's best families, is rich, successful—you can't do better."

"I—" She shook her head, dread mixing with astonishment. Because he wasn't kidding.

Oh my God, *he wasn't kidding.*

"Dad, you can't just arrange marriages like this is feudal England. I'm a grown woman fully capable of choosing men to date and one to eventually marry. And when I do, his credentials will include more than the number of zeros in his bank account or how far back he can trace his roots," she argued. Wondering why in the world she was actually having this discussion.

"As your father, I have a vested interest in who you marry and who enters our family. This isn't just about you," he persisted. The steely note in his voice had horror coiling around her rib cage.

"Since it will be me pledging my future to someone, living with them, sleeping with them and having kids by them, I would say it's most definitely about me," she snapped, unable to contain her irritation... and growing panic.

His gaze narrowed on her, and he stalked across the room back to the fireplace, where he deliberately set his drink down on the stone mantel. "I have cared for you, provided for you, worked hard and sacrificed for you. There is no better judge of who you should call a husband than me. And that includes you."

You did it all for you. *For your pride, your ego, your never satisfied need for more.*

The scream filled her head. Only sheer will and a deeply rooted respect for his role as her father prevented the words from tumbling past her lips.

"Now," he continued, "after all the trouble I went through to secure this arrangement, you *will* be at your best. You *will* impress him tonight. He has connections that far surpass business. Thanks to me, you will be welcomed into Boston society and have all kinds of doors opened to you. To both of us. I won't allow you to mess that up."

"And what about kindness? Affection? Love? I don't deserve that kind of marriage? Like you had with Mom?" she whispered.

"And you see how well that turned out," he snapped. "I'm doing you a favor, Devon. Enter a relationship based on mutual benefits and common ground and if, God forbid, you end up a widow, you won't be left devastated and broken. Remember that, Devon. Keep your heart out of this. And you will have the best life I could ever gift you with."

"Dad, are you listening to yourself?" she demanded,

disbelief and bone-deep sorrow pulsing in her. "You can't possibly mean any of that." She shook her head. Yes, her mother's death had changed him. But this much? When had he become so...cold? So hard-hearted? "Sorry, Dad. I can't do it. You might think an arranged marriage is some kind of blessing, but to me it would be hell. I won't marry a stranger."

And what kind of man would agree to this archaic and self-serving nonsense? What did he expect from her? More to the point, what did her father promise him to get him to agree to this farce? If he really was one of the country's most eligible bachelors, then he should have his pick of women. Devon was a realist; she was kind, smart and a hard worker. But she wasn't the most connected, the wealthiest or the most beautiful. Why her?

"You'll do it, Devon," he snarled. "Because I've raised you, sacrificed for you."

"You did those things because you're my father," she replied, anger at his attempt at emotional blackmail coursing through her. "It's what fathers do."

"And daughters put their families first," he snapped. Pausing, he drew his shoulders back, visibly calming himself. Turning, he picked up his glass again and drank from it. When he faced her again, he slid his free hand into his pants pocket and quietly studied her. "Devon, you're going along with this—"

"No, sorry. But I'm not," she interjected.

He continued speaking as if she hadn't interrupted. "Because if you don't, I'll make sure the funding for that precious community center you love will be rescinded. And I'll make the rounds with other donors and convince them the center is a bad investment. You know as well as I do that there isn't a lack of charities where that money can be applied."

Anger, so hot, so rich she could taste it, broke over her. A tremble quaked through her, and in that moment, she hated him. For rendering her powerless. For reducing her worth to no more than an asset he could trade or cash in. For who he'd become.

Guilt and shame crashed into her, a churning deluge that damn near drowned her. What kind of daughter harbored those thoughts about the man who'd brought her into this world? Before her mother died, she'd hugged Devon close and made her promise to look after her father. Logically, Devon understood that her mother hadn't meant to place such a burden on a ten-year-old. But that vow had chained Devon to her father all these years. At twenty-six, she still remained with him, worried about how hard he pushed himself, driven by invisible demons.

"Would you really take away my job, the place I care most about?" she asked quietly.

He scoffed, flicking off her question as if batting away an annoying gnat. "I've told you repeatedly you don't need that job. You have your choice of volunteer committees where you could actually bring about change by fundraising and forging relationships with people who matter. But instead, you insist on taking a menial position that anyone with a rudimentary degree could work at. So yes, I would take that away, if you force my hand. Gladly. Because it would be for your own good, which you're too stubborn to see."

Her father was right—this wasn't just about her. Not since he put the future of the community center on the line. For four years, it hadn't only been a place to utilize her bachelor's degree in urban studies and her master's in social work—it was also a haven. The staff, the children, the senior citizens and their loved ones had become surrogates for the family she'd left behind in New Jersey. So how selfish would it be of her to rip funding out from under them just to save herself? Employees would have to be let go. The center would lose programs that served all the demographics of the community, not just youths, but before- and after-school care, and elderly care.

No, she wouldn't allow her father to harm the center and all the people it assisted and employed.

She also wouldn't let him determine her future. As he'd taught her, she'd play the game. For now. But somehow, she'd find a way out of this sham. How? No clue. Yet.

"Fine, Dad," she said, curling her fingers around the back of the couch, steadying herself against the foreboding that swept through her. As if with those two words she'd sealed her fate. "You win. If you leave the community center alone, I'll go along with this."

"Marriage, Devon," he stated, a vein of steel threading through his voice. "Not only will you marry the man I've handpicked for you, but you'll make him believe this is what you want. You'll convince him your dream is to be his wife. This discussion stays here between us, Devon. And I mean that. Do you understand?"

"Of course, Dad," she murmured, the placid tone belying her death grip on the furniture. "You want me to begin my future on a lie. Got it."

"Devon," he barked, but the peal of the doorbell broke off what would have undoubtedly been a scathing dressing-down. He scowled. "Who is that? Are you expecting someone?"

She didn't have a chance to reply before their housekeeper appeared in the room's entrance. "Sir, I'm sorry to interrupt you and Ms. Devon, but there's a gentleman at the door. He claims you are expecting him. I placed him in the formal living room—"

"Since I'm practically family, I decided not to stand on formalities," drawled a dark, silken voice of velvet and grit.

She knew that voice.

Heard that voice in her dreams.

No. Oh God, *no. It couldn't be.*

Slowly, she pivoted, as if delaying what her clamoring heart and the heat pooling low in her belly already concluded.

But neither her ears, her heart nor the desire lighting her up like the Boston skyline were lying to her. Only one man had caused her body to tighten with a peculiar combination of anticipation, lust, excitement and trepidation. And he stood in her home.

Cain Farrell.

Delight exploded within her, and the beginnings of a tremulous smile tilted the corners of her mouth. She took a small step forward, but then his words penetrated her shock.

Since I'm practically family...

Wait. She jerked to a halt.

He couldn't possibly mean...

She shot a glance over her shoulder at her father, and the smug smirk confirmed the dread yawning wider in her chest. In her soul.

She returned her attention to the silent, brooding man standing feet from her. Instinct warned her that between him and her father, he was the one who presented the most danger. Not physically. Even though his tall, wide-shouldered frame seemed to shrink the spacious room to a cubbyhole, she didn't fear him using his size against her.

No, the danger he posed was much more nebulous, intangible.

Swallowing, she again moved toward him, his name hovering on her tongue. But he shifted his gaze from her father to her. And once more, she jerked to a halt.

Those wolf eyes didn't gleam with humor or admiration or even bemusement.

Loathing.

He stared at her with pure, unadulterated loathing.

Cain Farrell hated her.

And she couldn't blame him.

Not one bit.

Five

Her.

Betrayal, razor sharp, bit into him. Ridiculous and inexplicable how deep the hurt and bitterness pierced. He'd spoken with her for all of ten minutes, didn't even know her last name. And yet…

Yet, he'd dreamed about her. Built her up in his mind to be this paragon of kindness, innocence and… decency. A paragon of all the things he'd believed were gone from this world.

God, he was such a fool.

He'd thought it would be impossible to be as enraged as he'd been in his office with Gregory. Wrong.

He'd been so wrong.

Before, he'd been enraged.

Now, he was *furious*.

She'd played him. Had probably arranged that little meeting in his mother's garden. Well, she deserved a goddamn award for the performance. He'd fallen for it. Had she and her father laughed about him afterward? Congratulated themselves on a job well done?

Anger, fueled by disillusionment and humiliation, poured through him like gasoline. And the phony shock and hint of sadness in her emerald eyes was the match that had his control on the verge of detonating. No wonder Gregory Cole's gaze had seemed familiar to him. He'd stared into those same green, deceptive depths before.

Never again. Never again would he believe what shone from those beautiful, treacherous eyes or those sensual, lying lips.

"Cain, this is a surprise. We were expecting you for dinner," Gregory greeted, smiling as he crossed the room, his arm outstretched to shake Cain's hand.

Was he fucking kidding?

Cain stared down at Gregory's palm until the other man lowered his arm back to his side. Crimson stained Gregory's cheekbones and twin lines bracketed his mouth.

"You may be blackmailing me into marrying your daughter, but don't for one second believe that makes us friends. Or even friendly. I warned you what you would get from me. My name. That's it. Not small talk. Not pleasantries. And not dinners. I came by to meet the person so desperate for a man and a foothold in society that she would allow her father to take criminal measures on her behalf." He swung his regard back to Devon, gratified to see she'd wiped that attempt at genuine emotion from her face. It didn't fit her. "And now that I have met her, I want a moment alone with my fiancée. Since you've gone to so much trouble, you don't mind, do you, Devon?"

Gregory glanced sharply at his daughter, who did an applause-worthy job of appearing guilty. Her thick eyelashes lowered, and she didn't meet her father's gaze. Nice try, but keeping up pretenses of innocence was unnecessary. That ship had sailed. Just being here in the same room with her father solidified that she was a willing accomplice.

"Devon?" Gregory barked, and though Cain harbored no sympathy for her, he clenched his jaw against the impulsive need to order Cole to watch his tone.

"I have no problem speaking with you," she murmured, ignoring her father and addressing Cain.

The dense fringe of lashes lifted, and he glimpsed determination in her stare. She would need that determination dealing with him. Because he intended to grant her and her father the same amount of mercy they'd offered him.

None.

"Well, I have a problem," Gregory snapped.

"And I don't care," Cain said, not bothering to hide his impatience and disgust for the man. "Either we talk now, or I leave."

Gregory's expression tightened, his facial bones stark under his skin. Cain read the fury in his glare, the taut pull of his mouth and the tense set of his shoulders.

And he relished it.

"Fine," Gregory eventually growled. "Twenty minutes."

He stalked from the room, and Cain snorted. If that was supposed to be a show of parental concern, Gregory had failed. A man like him didn't care about something as tender as his daughter's feelings or well-being. Hell, he was trading both for more business, more wealth and an entrance into an inner social circle whose doors had been closed to him. No, more likely he worried about not controlling the situation.

Welcome to the fucking club.

As soon as he disappeared, Cain turned back to Devon...and slow clapped, the gesture condescending.

"Well done," he drawled. "I congratulate you on a stellar performance. Your father must be proud of his star pupil."

"Cain, I'm sorry," she murmured.

He snorted. "You'll have to be more specific. For what? Lying in wait for me during my father's funeral? For tag-teaming with your father to extort me?"

For making a fool out of me? For making me believe I saw sweetness in you? For every sweaty, hot night I woke up hard and aching for a woman who didn't exist?

As the too-vulnerable questions whispered through his mind, he locked his jaw and strode past her to the bar he'd spied when he'd entered the well-appointed room. Part of him detested partaking of anything that belonged to Gregory Cole—and that included his daughter.

But the other half acknowledged that this conversation required a drink. And that he needed to keep his hands busy—before they acted of their own accord and mapped the dangerous curves showcased by the simple long-sleeved T-shirt and dark, hip-hugging jeans.

She was like the lily of the valley—elegant, sweet, virginal. But if ingested, poisonous.

Tearing his gaze from her, he poured a finger of Scotch into a glass and brought it to his lips. He downed the alcohol in one swallow. Closing his eyes, he welcomed the smooth burn. It warmed him, spreading as it hit his stomach. Anything to distract him from wondering if those beautiful breasts would spill over his hands if he cupped her. If her nipples would be a slightly lighter hue than her caramel-colored hair, or would they be a deep rose.

He poured another drink to try and convince himself he didn't care.

Yeah. Not enough Scotch in the world for that.

"Cain, I know you won't believe me, but I'm sorry you've been dragged into this…" She faltered, not finishing the sentence, and he threw back the second drink, slamming the glass down as the Scotch hit the back of his throat.

"Into this shit show, you mean?" he supplied, arching a brow. "You offer up that pretty apology as if you have nothing to do with this. As if your selfish demands aren't screwing with my life," he growled. "I don't have much of a choice here, but you? All you have to do is tell your father no, that you won't go along with it. But you're not going to do that, are you, Devon? Not when both of you have dollar signs in your eyes."

She swept her hands over her hair, dragging away

the few loose strands that had escaped her ponytail. She turned away from him, giving him her profile to study. The high forehead. The impudent tilt of her nose. The top-heavy bow of her mouth. In another era, artists would've competed to paint the elegance of her features and lushness of her body. Now, in this more material-istic and shallow society, beauty like hers earned criti-cism instead of praise. Which just proved society was dumb as well as blind.

Her curves, dips and hollows would lure men to their downfall like currents sweeping ships to crash against jagged rocks.

Well, screw that. He might find himself shackled to her, but damn if he would be a casualty to his dick.

"No," she said, facing him again, her chest lifting and falling on the audible breath she inhaled. "I can't back out of it."

He'd expected the answer—had known the answer. And yet it still slammed into him, the knowledge re-verberating through him like an earthquake. As if there had been a small part of him hanging on to the hope that he'd misjudged her. That he hadn't been so damn *wrong*.

How many times would he be a fool for this woman?

Never. Again.

"Even though the thought of chaining myself to a gold-digging bitch and her bottom-feeder father makes my skin crawl, part of me is glad you said that," he murmured.

Ignoring the jerk of her chin and the slight recoil of her body, he stalked closer, eating up the distance he'd placed between them. She shifted backward, but the couch prevented her from going any farther. And he took advantage of it. Trapping her body between his and the fussy piece of furniture. He stopped just short of pressing his chest to hers, but near enough that her scent—a sultry combination of honey and sharper citrus notes—teased him. Taunted him. Steeling himself against it, he cocked his head to the side and studied her.

Not caring that both his open inspection and the infiltration of her personal space sped past rude and parked next to inappropriate. There was nothing *appropriate* about any of this.

"Because now, when I do everything in my power to make your very existence a living hell, you'll know exactly why you'll receive no mercy from me. I hope you enjoyed that moment of satisfaction when your father told you he got me on the hook. Because that's the last time you'll feel anything close to it again."

"Does it make you feel better to threaten me?" she asked, and he resented her calm, the evenness of her voice. Like he was the only one drowning in emotion.

God, he wanted—*needed*—her to go under with him.

"Yes," he replied, and she blinked at his blunt candor. "But you don't need to bother with this act on my behalf, sweetheart. Pretending to be the sweet, concerned, *honest* woman who introduced herself in the garden—it must've been tiring, maintaining that charade. No need to keep it up when I can see right through you." He lifted a hand and gently dragged the backs of his fingers down her cheek, imitating and mocking the touch he'd surrendered to before. Before he'd discovered that soft heart was actually made of stone and yearning for large denominations. "That might be the one thing you'll enjoy about our marriage. The freedom of no pretense. I'm going into this already knowing you're a coldhearted, greedy social climber who would do anything to get what she wants."

Fire flashed in those eyes and, God help him, excitement twisted with anger in his blood, creating an unholy union. Desire—he recognized it, acknowledged it. He might despise everything Devon stood for, but that didn't prevent lust from locking him in its jaws, from hardening his body to the point of pain.

"Good girl," he purred, rubbing his thumb over that slightly fuller top lip. He pressed gently, testing the texture, the give. Her gasp bathed his skin, and before he could check it, he bowed his head over hers, their foreheads almost touching. "There it is. I want to see that fire you hide behind a purity we both know doesn't suit you."

She slid her arms between them, flattening her hands on his chest and shoving him away. He shifted backward, and the bitter twist of her lips telegraphed what they both knew—she'd slipped away only because he'd allowed it.

"You don't know me," she snapped, crossing her arms over her chest.

On another person, the gesture would've struck him as self-protective. But this wasn't another person; it was Devon Cole, and as he'd learned, she was a master at portraying herself to be something she wasn't.

"Ten minutes in my company doesn't make you an expert on who I am. And don't flatter yourself. You might think you're this wonderful catch that I have to plot and scheme to trap, but you're not the only one sacrificing. Contrary to what you believe, this isn't all about you."

"Prove it," he said. "Call your father in here and put an end to this." When she didn't answer, didn't move toward the door, his lips curved into a mocking, cynical twist. "So much for your pretty speech. Righteous indignation doesn't become you, sweetheart."

Sighing, she pinched the bridge of her nose. "Cain, listen. I—"

"No," he interrupted. Unbidden and without his conscious permission, his gaze raked down her body again. His blood pounded in his veins, his cock. She was untrustworthy, a liar, and he detested that his body could betray him. Could make him weak for her. The fear of that weakness coated his voice in ice as he met her wide eyes. "You listen. Because I want it crystal clear what you're in for if you and your father go ahead with blackmailing me. Like I told your father, you'll get my name, but here's what you won't have from me. Peace. Happiness. Fidelity. I refuse to curb my lifestyle for you. Your father might receive the perceived benefits of me as a son-in-law, but you'll be the one to pay the price. Day in and day out. Consider that, Devon. And decide if it's worth it. I promise you. It isn't."

He pivoted and strode from the room, unable to spend another moment staring into those bottomless eyes. Eyes that had darkened with an emotion he refused to attribute to her. Remorse.

No, she wasn't capable of that.

And he wouldn't fall for her act again. She'd duped him once, had made him believe. Had played him.

She wouldn't receive a second chance.

Six

Devon stepped from the elevator onto the executive floor of Farrell International. Except for soft murmurings and the muted click-clack of fingers flying over keyboards, a silence not unlike a church permeated the expansive area. Her heels sank into the plush dark blue carpet, and on either side of her, artwork that wouldn't have been out of place in a museum graced the dark wood walls. Wide, circular desks manned by professionally dressed men and women dotted the floor, guarding closed double doors that bore gold nameplates.

Power. Wealth. Before arriving here today, she hadn't known they possessed a smell. Lemon verbena and fresh cedar. And something more elusive, indefinable.

It was that something that clung to Cain.

She'd inhaled it when he'd pressed against her in

her father's living room. When he'd surrounded her. Touched her. Let her feel the imprint of his thumb on her mouth. After he'd left, she'd swept her tongue over her lip, his caress a phantom weight on her flesh. And even though his hand had long left her, she tasted him. That same scent. Dark. Sensual.

Exciting.

Lord. She barely stopped herself from spreading her fingers over her stomach. What did it say about her that when he'd crowded her, glared at her with those wolf eyes—hell, *threatened her*—she hadn't felt fear? No, it hadn't been that emotion pumping through her blood, tingling her nipples into taut tips, swirling low in her belly…wetting the flesh between her legs.

It'd been lust.

Pure and simple.

Well, if anything that greedy and clawing could be pure.

She'd experienced desire before; she was a twenty-six-year-old woman, and she'd been with a few men. Even enjoyed sex. The connection, the intimacy, the physical bonding—she wasn't ashamed to admit she took pleasure in the act. Especially when love was involved. But it was love that had her steeped in the middle of a year-long sexual drought.

Donald Harrison had been an associate quickly moving up the ranks of her father's firm. When he'd approached her at a business event, she'd been flattered and attracted to him. Why not? With his dark blond hair, deep brown eyes and athletic build, he'd drawn many appreciative glances from women and men alike. But his interest had been solely focused on her. He'd showered her in compliments, gifts and affection. Her father hadn't been thrilled about her relationship with a "mere associate," but Devon hadn't cared. She'd loved Donald. Could see them sharing a future together.

Which had made her discovery so shattering. He'd been using her only to climb the corporate ladder in her father's company.

It'd been a year since her father had slid that file across the dining room table. He'd chosen breakfast to break the news to her. One task to get out of the way over coffee before his day started. He'd nonchalantly eaten a perfectly cooked omelet while she'd read about Donald's fiancée, the house they'd just bought in Charlestown, even a picture of the engagement ring. And while her heart had been crushed, her father had lectured her about not being astute enough to recognize a "chaser" when she encountered one. About being too naive to recognize a man who desired her wealth and connections rather than her.

The irony didn't elude her.

Then, she'd been the one used for upward mobility.

Now, she was doing the using. Not willingly. But in the end, it didn't matter.

Not to her father. And certainly not to Cain Farrell.

At least she entered into this arrangement with her eyes wide open, not blinded by sentiments such as love and loyalty. Cain harbored none for her; the only emotion he possessed when it came to her was hate. And though that stung—God, glimpsing the loathing in his eyes, hearing it drip from his voice had been scalding—maybe, it was for the best.

As of now, she hadn't devised a way to escape her father's plans. Which meant for the foreseeable future, she was trapped, unable to back out and unable to confess to Cain why she had to go through with this.

But given her completely inconvenient desire for Cain, his disdain for her might save her from herself, from her untrustworthy heart. She'd confused physical attraction with love before. But just one mocking caress down her cheek from Cain had stoked her lust hotter than sex with Donald. So if she didn't guard herself against Cain...

She couldn't do anything as foolish as allow herself to be vulnerable with him. Lowering her guard would be like opening the cage door to a prowling lion.

In other words, stupid as hell.

"Can I help you?" the statuesque brunette behind a large gleaming desk asked Devon as she approached.

Devon glanced at the closed double doors behind the desk. For a moment, panic seized her. Cain had requested her presence with a terse text message, but he hadn't included why. What awaited her? The first step in his plan to begin making her existence a "living hell"?

Anxiety should be the only emotion quivering through her at the thought of his threat. Not anticipation. Damn sure not excitement.

Maybe she was as twisted as Cain believed her to be.

"Hello," she said, smiling at the executive assistant whose nameplate proclaimed her to be Charlene Gregg. "Cain Farrell is expecting me. Devon Cole."

Charlene nodded. "Yes, he told me to send you in as soon as you arrived. Just through those doors."

"Thank you." Devon offered her another smile, hoping it didn't betray the nerves rattling inside her.

Inhaling a deep breath, she walked forward, chin tilted upward, shoulders squared. One of her mother's favorite sayings had been "Faith it until you make it," her twist on the old axiom. Well, Devon would have faith that she wouldn't appear like a lamb heading into the slaughter until she actually didn't feel like one.

No telling how long that would take.

Pulling open the door, she stepped into Cain's inner sanctum. Stalling, she surveyed the spacious office. Glass comprised two of the four walls, and tasteful masculine furniture of wood and leather dotted a sitting area. Instead of the beautiful artwork that decorated the outer office, huge framed black-and-white photographs of historic Boston adorned the walls. Faneuil Hall. The *Appeal to the Great Spirit* statue in front of the Museum of Fine Arts. The Bunker Hill Monument. The Old North Church. The lighting, the imagery, the tone of the photos—they were all stunning. And seemed out of place in the office of a merciless billionaire.

Her gaze jerked toward Cain.

And immediately she regretted the impulse.

The stirring of curiosity flickered then died in her chest. His cold, narrowed stare extinguished it. Not even two minutes later, and she'd already broken a rule she'd set for herself. Guard against any emotion with Cain. And that included curiosity. Because it was the gateway drug that led to other emotions—interest, wonder, compassion, need...

Do better, she snapped at herself.

Then she deliberately conjured the memory of the heartache that had nearly ripped her in half after discovering Donald's lies. She embraced that ache, let it soak into her skin, her bones. She'd hold on to it so she wouldn't slip again.

"You summoned me here," she said, injecting the calm nonchalance that had abandoned her the second she entered the downtown Boston skyscraper of Farrell International's offices.

That was one lesson she'd come away with from their meeting at her home a week earlier.

Never show weakness in front of this man.

"Can I always expect this kind of pliancy during our marriage?" he mocked. "Submissiveness in a woman isn't something I'm usually attracted to, but for you I could make an exception."

"Making allowances for me already?" She shook her head, tsking, even as a voice inside her head yelled, *What the hell are you doing? Don't poke the beast!* "You're setting a bad precedent. And you know how women like me will take full advantage of that."

He didn't reply, but his intense scrutiny stroked over her, from the center part of her drawn-back hair, down the straight lines of her dress to her dark green stiletto heels. When she'd donned the green-and-white-striped shirt with the big bow tie at the neck and the emerald pencil skirt, the outfit had seemed both professional and flattering. Now, with that blue-gray gaze on her, she fought not to check if she'd left a button or two loose or if her skirt skimmed too tightly over her hips.

His eyes lifted to hers, and her words—*"take full advantage of that"*—seemed to resonate in the office. Suddenly, instead of referring to his permissiveness, it sounded as if she were offering him something else to exploit. Herself.

A dull throb of heat beat low in her belly, edging farther south. Settling deep between her legs. Her mind railed against the implication of her words, demanding she clear up her meaning. But her body, mainly the flesh between her legs, approved of this new plan of action.

She was in trouble.

"While I appreciate the sudden display of honesty, that's not why I asked you here." He picked up a tablet, tapped the screen a few times then rounded his desk, extending the device toward her.

Primal survival instincts cried out that she retreat, hide from the ultimate predator in the room. But pride—foolish, self-destructive pride—kept her feet rooted. She might not have any intention of going through with this disaster of a marriage if she could find a way out of it, but she also didn't intend to start any relationship, no matter how short-lived, cowering from him.

She'd lost her mother as a child, and in every way that mattered, her father, too. And she'd survived it, become a woman who could weather a storm and come out stronger on the other side. Battered maybe, but not beaten.

And no way in hell would she allow Cain Farrell to accomplish what fate hadn't managed to do.

She shifted forward instead of backing up, meeting him halfway and accepting the tablet. Her fingertips brushed his, but she kept her gaze glued to the screen, absorbing the tingling shock against her skin. She might not be able to do anything about her body's reaction to this man, but she didn't have to let him see the effect he had on her.

Focusing her attention on the device, she scanned the website he'd pulled up, recognizing it as one of the more popular columns that featured on-dits about Boston society. Huh. He didn't strike her as the kind of man who gave a damn about gossip. She frowned, but kept reading. Moments later, she sucked in an abrupt, hard breath.

What the... He *hadn't*...

But dammit, he had.

"I—" she stuttered, humiliation and anger burning through her like a blowtorch. "I didn't—"

"Didn't what?" Cain cut her off, the ice in his tone freezing her. "Didn't leak the news about our nonexistent engagement to the press? Didn't give an exclusive to this little gossip rag?"

"I didn't do it," she insisted, her fingers so tight around the tablet it was a wonder the screen didn't crack under the pressure. "I wouldn't without your agreement."

"So you'd have me believe you grew morals overnight?" He arched an eyebrow. "If you didn't leak this, then your father did. Not that it matters. The only thing that does matter is that I hadn't found the opportunity to tell my mother about our—" he paused, his lips twisting into a cruel sneer "—*arrangement* yet. Instead of hearing it from her son, she read it in that silly column. Do you know what it's like to look your mother in the eye and lie to her, Devon? Do you know how dirty that makes you feel?"

"No," she whispered. "I don't know what that's like. My mother died when I was ten."

Cain stiffened, and silence pounded in the room like a heartbeat. Throbbed with tension, with the ache of loss. At least on her part. What would her mother say about this situation? Would they even be here if she was alive? Would her father be the man he'd become?

So many what-ifs…

"You understood the pain I was feeling, you mentioned that in the garden," he murmured, his gaze roaming over her face, searching. She wanted to hide from that incisive scrutiny. He couldn't have her memories, couldn't have her pain. "I'm sorry about your mother, Devon. Mothers…" An emotion so stark, so dark, that the breath locked in her lungs flashed in his eyes. In the next instant, it disappeared, but she hadn't imagined it. Not when her chest echoed with it. "Mothers are special. And I'm sorry you lost yours."

"It's been sixteen years."

"You still miss her."

"I do," she rasped, the admission slipping from her without her permission.

She blinked against the sting of tears. *No, dammit.* No weakness. God, there wasn't much hope for her to survive this whole thing if she couldn't stop breaking her rules with this man.

Clearing her throat, she shoved the tablet at him. "Here." She barely waited for him to accept it, being careful that they didn't touch again. Smoothing her damp palms down her hips, she strode over to one of the windows and stared out at the view of downtown Boston and beyond.

A king. He was a king all the way up here at the top floor of this lofty building. Did that make them all peasants in his sight? Or did that make him distant and lonely, a prince in a gilded tower of his own making?

"I didn't place that gossip in the column. But I will apologize for my father's actions. Not that it will make much difference now."

"No, it won't," he agreed, the ice returning to his tone. "I hadn't decided what story to tell my mother about an impending marriage, much less why I haven't introduced her to a woman I've been seeing long enough to make my wife." His woodsy, fresh scent, heated by that big body, reached out to her, teasing her. Teasing her with what she craved, but her mind—her heart— knew it would be lethal for her to partake. "I would cut my own heart out before breaking my mother's. And telling her I'm entering the same loveless prison she endured with my father would accomplish that. So I had to lie and convince her I've fallen in love," he bit out. A caustic note hardened those words, telegraphing his opinion of falling in love with her. "And with the choice of hurting my mother or continuing this charade, I'm going to sell the hell out of it. Which means even though you see a walking dollar bill when you look at me, you better scrape together all your superb acting skills and pretend I'm the man you can't live without when you're in front of her. And for whoever else we need to convince so the truth never gets back to her."

The weight of her father's machinations landed hard in her chest. From one moment to the next, she couldn't breathe. As if all his schemes, lies and betrayals shrank the room, and she battled claustrophobia, scratching and clawing to escape. His needs, his goals, his greed demanded a price, but it was her and Cain who had to pay the cost.

And it was high.

"Mr. Farrell, Laurence Reese from Liberty Photography is here for your appointment." Charlene's voice dragged Devon from the dark hole she'd been sliding down, and she glanced at Cain's desk phone, almost grateful.

"Consider this your first casting call," Cain said, and she blinked at the enigmatic statement, turning to watch him stride toward his desk.

"What?" she asked, confused.

He glanced over his shoulder at her, a cold, humorless smile curving his mouth. "Our engagement photos." Before she could reply—hell, *if* she could reply—he pressed a button on the phone. "Send him in, Charlene. Thank you." He started toward his office door but paused at her side. Lowering his head, he murmured, "I want every person who looks at these photos to swoon and fall in love with the idea of us. To crown us the next fucking Harry and Meghan. So better bring your A game, sweetheart."

His lips grazed the rim of her ear on each word, and

she fought not to betray how even that slight caress sent desire spiraling through her.

Only when he continued across the room did she turn around, inhaling a gulp of air, her lungs on fire from the breath she'd been holding. Her heart thudded against her rib cage, a primal rhythm that echoed in her head, drowning out the conversation between Cain and the tall, thin man who entered the office. They shook hands, and when Laurence Reese glanced in her direction, she forced a smile to her lips. Though it felt brittle and phony, the gesture must've passed muster because the photographer returned her smile, his brown eyes warm.

Behind him, a crew poured into the office toting equipment. Devon hung back as the photographer and his assistants worked. In short order, they had cameras, tripods and reflective umbrellas set up. Cables snaked across the floor and Laurence even had his people set up a green screen on one side of the room. They performed in a well-organized unit, and it wasn't long before the photographer, camera hanging around his neck, directed them to stand in front of the window.

With Cain's permission, several people had moved his massive desk out of the way, and Devon could imagine the picture would reflect a power couple with all of Boston stretched behind them like their kingdom.

And they said a picture was worth a thousand words. Right.

All of theirs would be lies.

"How about we start with you, Mr. Farrell, behind Ms. Cole. If you'll wrap your arms around her…" Laurence instructed, lifting his camera over his head.

Damn. *Damndamndamn.*

She couldn't move. Couldn't breathe. Cain. With his arms wrapped around her. She stiffened, tension starting at her toes and racing like a lightning bolt up her body until she stood so tight, one tap would probably send her tumbling forward. And shattering into pieces.

It occurred to her that the first time Cain embraced her would be just for the sake of the camera and public consumption. There was something seedy about it. And yet, a secret part of her that she'd buried so deep she barely acknowledged it hungered to be held by this man. Yearned to know how his body would cover her shelter her. Protect her. And that part, which had been wounded by rejection, by deceit, by blows to its self-esteem, wasn't picky about how it happened.

A hard wall of expensive wool and muscle pressed to her back. She gasped, that initial contact smashing her paralysis. An electrical current zigzagged through her, making her body jerk. But strong, toned arms slid under hers and circled her waist, controlling the involuntary motion.

"Shh, easy," Cain rumbled in her ear, his head lowered over hers. To the photographer, it probably appeared as if he were affectionately nuzzling her. "You love my arms around you, remember? Want my hands on your body."

Oh God.

Her lashes fluttered, and she sank her teeth into her bottom lip, trapping the moan that crawled up her throat. His words elicited hot, erotic images of his arms holding her close in another setting. One with a wide bed, twisted sheets, air thick with the musky scent of sex. One where those big long-fingered hands swept over her bare skin, cupped her heavy breasts, pinched her beaded nipples…dipped between her trembling thighs…

"Yes, perfect," Laurence praised, his camera snapping away in rapid-fire succession. Startled, Devon lifted her hands, cupping them over Cain's. He immediately intertwined their fingers, and she couldn't help but look down. Their fingers looked like puzzle pieces finding homes; it struck her as beautiful. And for a stupid, nonsensical moment, tears stung her eyes. "Beautiful," the photographer murmured, edging closer to them, camera whirring and clicking. "Now look at me."

They followed his instructions for the next thirty minutes, and the half hour flew by in a haze of simmering desire and embarrassment. She tried to pretend it didn't faze her every time Cain cupped her elbow or pressed his chest to hers or curved an arm around her waist. Tried to act as if this was business as usual for a woman in love. And all the while she secretly prayed that the invasive and all-too-perceptive camera lens didn't capture the dueling emotions waging an epic battle inside her—uncertainty, lust, vulnerability, a ravenous hunger that surpassed the physical, a hunger for the closeness they were making a sham of.

A hunger for pretense to be reality.

Oh God, she needed this to be done. And not just the shoot, but this mess her father had dropped her into. She was a motherless child, a neglected daughter, a rejected woman. In other words, so starved for love that she'd easily—willingly—turn to this man for affection. For scraps of kindness, even knowing they were faked for the eyes of others...

A sob clawed at her throat, desperation squeezing her, trapping her like the restricting sleeves of a straitjacket—

Cain strode over to the photographer to view some of the pictures on the digital screen, and she took advantage of the reprieve. Whirling around, she bolted back to the window. She stared sightlessly out, gulping in huge breaths and shoving back the edges of panic.

No. No, dammit.

The admonishment rang in her head, bringing her back from the emotional edge.

She wasn't weak. She wasn't fragile or damaged. Donald hadn't broken her; she'd come out stronger for that. Smarter and not so naive. And Cain wouldn't finish what Donald had started.

She wouldn't allow him to.

"One more pose, if you don't mind," Laurence said, switching out cameras with one of his assistants. "How do you feel about a shot with a kiss?" He smiled. "Only if you're comfortable with it, though."

She turned from the window to find Cain's hooded, blue-gray gaze on her. Her breath snagged in her throat and inside her head, the "hell no" bounced around, deafening. But she remained silent, returning that stare, certain he would decline. He didn't want to kiss her. Hell, he'd pretty much told her their marriage, if they progressed that far, would be a cold one and she would have to find pleasure in someone else's bed—as he planned to do. So, surely he would shoot down this suggestion.

Any minute now.

"Where do you want us?" Cain asked Laurence, not removing his scrutiny from her.

That was *not* a refusal.

"In front of the green screen," he instructed them.

Cain slowly stretched his arm toward her, palm up. She stared at it, unmoving. But realizing everyone waited on her, she forced her feet forward...and slid her hand across his. Inexplicably, the nerves battering her calmed. Which made zero sense because he *was* the cause of those nerves.

Jesus, she was in so much trouble.

He quietly led her across the room to stand in front of the tall screen.

"Great," Laurence said. "Just be natural. Pretend we're not here."

Seriously? She could feel the eyes of every person in that room on her, on *them*. Her senses were so sharpened, she could hear their inhales, smell the clean notes of Laurence's Tom Ford aftershave. And if she glanced around, she'd glimpse the curiosity his team tried to hide behind their professionalism.

"Look at me," Cain murmured, low enough that it only carried to her ears. Unlike before when he'd issued orders, she couldn't help but obey. She lifted her gaze to his. "Your choice, Devon."

Her choice. He was giving her what had been stolen from him by her father and her, or so he believed.

And yet, he was offering a choice to her when he could just take.

A longing so deep it verged on pain filled her. A longing for the impossible. For time to reverse itself and all the events that had occurred—her father's interference, this forced engagement—to have never happened. That the impromptu meeting in the garden had been the impetus for a true romance and this moment they shared right now was genuine instead of a phony prop for an equally phony relationship.

But even God couldn't undo what was. They couldn't go back. She couldn't have that fairy tale. Still… Maybe she could have an element of that fantasy. A kiss. A bit of romance. A little tenderness. It wasn't too much to ask—too much to take.

She nodded.

Heat flashed in his eyes like dry lightning, lending his wolf eyes an almost eerie glow. And in that instant, she identified with prey. But instead of running away, she edged closer, tipping her head back. And if she resembled a creature exposing its vulnerable neck? Well, she credited it to the surreality of this moment.

Cain lifted his hand, but instead of cupping her face as she expected, he gripped the knot of hair twisted behind her head and tugged. Before the gasp could leave her lips, he'd freed the heavy, long strands. Shocked, she stared up at him, unable to contain her shiver as his blunt-tipped fingers dragged over her scalp then tangled in the wavy mass.

"I'd wondered," he murmured, echoing the same sentiment she'd uttered to him back in the garden when she'd first seen his eyes.

"You wondered what?" she whispered.

His inspection shifted from his hands buried in her hair to her eyes. The unfiltered desire in his gaze punched her in the chest and, reeling, she grasped at anything to steady herself in the wake of it. Him. His waist, to be more exact. Her fingers dug into the firm flesh that seemed to sear her through his white dress shirt. Instead of snatching her hands away from the heat, she burrowed closer. Clung harder.

He didn't answer her, but his hold on her thick strands tightened, and he pulled, tugging her head back farther. She shouldn't like that tiny pricks danced across her scalp. Shouldn't have loosed that low, needy sound that telegraphed exactly how much she liked it. But she did both, and when Cain's eyes narrowed, lust flaring brighter, hotter, she couldn't regret either.

She anticipated a conquering, passionate onslaught when the kiss came. But he surprised her again. He brushed his lips over hers. A gentle caress. A tender pursuit. And *oh God*. How she wished he'd overwhelmed her with lust. It would've been less confusing. Less devastating. She could've chalked up a hungry siege to lust and anger. Could've responded with the same. But this? She sighed. Or maybe whimpered. Either way, she melted. Her lips parted, and she couldn't resist the lure of the mouth that could appear so hard and cruel, but in truth was so incredibly soft. And sensual. And beautiful.

Canting her head to the side, he molded that gorgeous

mouth to hers, his tongue sweeping in, questioning even as he invited her to dance. And she did. No hesitation. With that decision, that surrender, the hunger she'd initially expected followed.

Now she understood why he'd gentled her first.

To prepare her for this.

He was a carnal marauder. A conqueror. And she, the willing captive. His for the seizing. And as he drove deep, licking, tangling and sucking, he razed a path of destruction through her senses. Through any past experience of what a kiss was or should be.

And she wanted more. *Needed* more.

"I think I have what I need." Laurence's voice, thick with amusement, penetrated the dense fog of lust that enshrouded her.

She stiffened, and Cain went rigid against her.

Mortification and despair roared to life within her, chasing away the passion that had blinded her to the fact that they had an audience. Mortification because she'd lost herself in his arms, had laid out her desire for him and in turn, offered him a tool to use against her. A damn novice's mistake. And in this game, she was far from a novice.

And despair because even now, anger crystallized his light gaze. At her, at himself—she didn't know. Not that it mattered. His remorse and disgust were plain for her to glimpse, and for a foolish instant, she mourned the loss of the tender, sensual stranger who had drawn both hunger and wonder from her with his kiss.

"Are we finished here, then?" Cain asked, stepping

away from her. The cold rushed in, wrapping her in its chilly embrace.

Pride constrained her arms at her sides, refusing to let her wrap them around herself in protection.

"Yes," Laurence nodded, apparently oblivious to the undercurrents of tension running between her and Cain. Or maybe he just interpreted it as sexual, considering the display they'd just put on. "I think you're going to be very pleased with the photos, Mr. Farrell."

Cain spoke with the photographer as he and his crew packed up, negating the need for her to engage in conversation. Thank God. Because she couldn't string two sentences together right now if she'd wanted to.

She glanced at Cain, scanning his tall, wide-shouldered frame, the powerful chest, flat stomach and long, muscular thighs. A sizzling coil of desire unfurled within her, and she raised her hand to her mouth, touching her trembling fingers to her tender lips.

As if he sensed the movement, Cain's regard shifted from Laurence to her. That gaze dropped to her mouth, and Devon dropped her arm as if caught mid-sin. Maybe thinking about wanting her fake fiancé to kiss the ever lovin' hell out of her wasn't on God's list of sins, but it was on hers.

Falling for the enemy might be a great romance trope, but this was real life. If she allowed Cain close, when he moved on, she wouldn't be left unscathed. And he would move on. If there was anything she'd learned since her mother's death it was that anyone could be ripped away at a whim.

Better she remember that the next time she wondered if his body looked as powerful without clothes as it did in them.

Starting now.

Seven

Cain remembered the first time he saw the *Mona Lisa*.
He'd been fifteen, and his father had taken him along on a business trip to Paris. It'd been boring as hell. For the five days they'd been in one of the most beautiful cities on earth, he'd spent ninety percent of it locked in conference rooms with his father and other businessmen. He hadn't cared about acquisitions or profits and losses. At fifteen, three things had consumed him: the Boston Red Sox, beating his best score on *Call of Duty* and getting to third base with Cassandra Ransom.

But then his father had allowed his assistant to take Cain on a tour of Paris. And he'd visited the Louvre and seen *her*. Mona Lisa. He'd spent at least an hour staring up at the painting of the mysterious Italian noblewoman with her dark beauty, wearing her enigmatic smile. The epitome of grace and yet, he always imagined that smile hinted at the woman's passion, joy, mischief. But especially her passion.

No flesh and blood woman had ever intrigued and captivated him as much as that piece of art.

Until now.

As Laurence and his staff exited his office, Cain ordered himself not to turn around and study the silent woman who hadn't moved from the wall where the green screen had stood. Not to turn and skim the interesting features only a blind man would call plain. Not to survey the breasts that had pressed against his chest, confirming every suspicion he'd had about their firmness and weight. Not to regard the almost dramatic flare of her full hips and the sensual thickness of her thighs. Not to stare at the mouth that had damn near brought him to his knees in front of an office full of people.

Jesus, the soft give of it, the heady, sultry taste of it—he'd lost control, forgotten about everything and everyone else except the woman sweetly surrendering to him, granting him her passion like a gift wrapped with a bow. That never happened with him, to him. *Ever.* And as he'd surfaced from the dark pool of lust, anger lit in him, but so did fear. Who had he become in those moments when he'd been drowning in her?

He'd suspected passion hot enough to reduce him to ash had existed behind that innocent demeanor. Had glimpsed it in the garden in those beautiful, deceptive eyes. And in the occasional flashes of temper and sarcasm. But to confirm it? To be on the receiving end of that lovely flame?

Goddamn. Since meeting her, his sleep had been disturbed with dreams of her. Now that he'd tasted her? He would be lucky if he ever slept again.

Clenching his jaw, he shut the door closed behind the last of the photography crew and crossed the room toward her. What else did she hide behind that Mona Lisa face? What else would he discover was a mask, a lie? If anything, today had shown him he could trust nothing about her.

The cherry on top of this shitty sundae would be for him to become a slave to his lust. To willfully turn a blind eye to her true nature just so he could be kissed by fire again. That's probably what her father intended.

Well, he was no one's puppet. Including his cock's.

"I should probably go—" Devon began.

"We need to—" he ground out simultaneously.

Whatever they would've said remained unfinished and hanging in the air as his door flew open and Achilles and Kenan strode in as if it was their office instead of his. Technically, they weren't wrong. Everything in this company belonged to them as much as it did him.

With that reminder, the bitterness he'd felt since the reading of Barron's will simmered to the surface. And spilled onto the men who'd barged into his life much as they'd done his office.

"Please, come in. My obviously closed door is always open," he drawled from between gritted teeth.

"Well, obviously," Kenan drawled back, a smile curving his mouth. His sharp gaze, identical to Cain's own, lit on Devon. "We heard a ridiculous rumor through the office gossip grapevine that you were in here with a photographer for an engagement photo shoot." He surveyed the room with an exaggerated turn of his head and body. "No photographer, but we do have a possible fiancée." Though his tone remained light and teasing, his gaze narrowed, and his smile hardened around the edges. "But that can't be true. Because surely Achilles and I wouldn't discover you were engaged to be married through the secretary pool? We would be devastated, right, Achilles?"

Achilles propped a shoulder against the wall, crossing his arms over his massive chest. "Devastated," he said, voice dry.

"Don't let the stoic face fool you. Inside, he's broken. As am I. So please clear it up for us, Cain. Is it true that you're getting married and we're the last to know? Like literally, behind the mail room clerk, last to know? And if so, why is it you didn't think it was any of our business? You know, being brothers and all."

"Brothers?" Devon gasped behind him.

He glanced over his shoulder, meeting her wide eyes. And sighed. "Devon, let me introduce you to my half brothers, Kenan Rhodes and Achilles Farrell." *Brothers* still seemed foreign on his tongue. Like a language he hadn't yet mastered. And wasn't sure he wanted to. "Kenan, Achilles, this is Devon Cole…my fiancée." It was a miracle he didn't choke on that title.

"A pleasure to meet you, Devon," Kenan greeted, his expression warming as he extended his hand toward her. Devon shook it, returning the warm gesture and smile.

And it was *not* jealousy that speared through Cain's rib cage at the pretty sight of it. He didn't *do* jealousy.

And did *not* covet that warmth or wish it was directed at him.

"Devon." Achilles dipped his head, the mouth surrounded by his thick beard remaining flat. The man could never be called emotive.

"It's nice to meet you both," Devon said. "And I'm sorry about Cain not sharing the news about our engagement with you. I asked him not to tell anyone until we announced it in the paper. Call it being superstitious, but I didn't want to jinx anything." She wrinkled her nose, the gesture adorable. And damn believable even as she lied with a straight face. "He was just indulging me."

"I'm trying to picture an indulgent Cain." Kenan cocked his head and squinted. "I kind of like the look on you, brother."

Across the room, Achilles snorted.

"If you two are finished with the nosy busybodies act, can I have a private moment with Devon, please?" Cain growled, his patience with the two men ending.

Kenan tsked, shaking his head. "We would be eternally grateful if you could do something about his manners while you're at it, Devon. Welcome to the family."

Kenan twisted *family* as if it were some kind of private joke. And maybe it was. To call them his "brothers" was more than a stretch—it neared a tall tale. Still, the asshole pressed a kiss to Devon's cheek and had the audacity to flash a grin at Cain before exiting the office. With a chin lift, Achilles unfolded himself and followed their younger brother out.

"Would it be totally inappropriate for me to start

singing 'Papa Was a Rolling Stone' right now?" Devon whispered.

Cain stared at her. Then snorted.

Instead of answering her question, though, he asked the one that had been plaguing him for the past few minutes. "Why did you lie to Kenan and Achilles?"

She shrugged. "I didn't want your brothers' feelings hurt because they believed you didn't tell them about the engagement. And I didn't want you to have to lie to another family member."

Astonishment whipped through him. Was this another trick, another tactic to make her appear less calculating than he knew her to be? It had to be. Otherwise, why did she care if Kenan or Achilles felt slighted by him? Why did it concern her at all?

He searched her face, her eyes for an ulterior motive. And as even as he did so, he couldn't get past how swollen her lips were—and how proud he felt that he was the cause.

"How are—" she faltered, glancing at the door. "You three are…"

"How are three men of different racial backgrounds, who are obviously strangers, brothers?" he finished for her.

She flushed but nodded.

"The miraculous story of the long-lost Farrell heirs was in the papers a couple of weeks ago. You didn't read about it?"

"It's better you find this out about me now instead of later. I honestly couldn't give a damn about business or society gossip. I go online to find out the latest reality

TV news and spoilers about my favorite Netflix shows. Everything else is detrimental to my ass."

He arched an eyebrow. "Detrimental to your…ass?"

"Yes." She nodded. "Reading all the crap that's going on right now in the world makes me either sad or angry. And I'm an emotional eater. So, all the chips, ice cream and chocolate go straight to my ass. Therefore, no upsetting internet searching for me."

He stared at her. Blinked. Then fought down the bark of laughter that pressed at his throat. *This* was the woman from the garden. Funny. Candid. Fucking adorable.

Note to self: Stop handing her opportunities to be adorable.

"Achilles and Kenan are my father's illegitimate children," he said, guiding them back to her original question…and away from his memories of those stolen moments in the garden. "I didn't discover their existence until after he died." He told her about the meeting and the terms of his father's will. "So we're forced to stay together for one year to save my family's company."

"I take it back," she whispered. "Your father wasn't a rolling stone. He was an asshole."

Again, the urge to laugh shoved at his throat. "Yes," he agreed. "Yes, he was."

She shook her head, the strands of that thick, gorgeous hair falling over her shoulder. He stared at the brown-and-gold mass. Curiosity had needled him into tugging it free from the bun during the photo shoot. He hadn't expected its heaviness, its softness. Or that it would slide over his skin, between his hands like a

caress. What would it feel like against his bare chest…
his thighs? Would it stream like a caramel waterfall to
her hips, stick to her damp skin while she rode him?

Lust shuddered through him.

He should never have touched her. Kissed her.

That had been a tactical error on his part. One he
had to avoid committing again at all costs.

She was a danger that needed blinking neon cau-
tion signs.

"Why would he do that? Wait until so late in life to
let you know you had brothers out there? Wouldn't you
have wanted to know about Achilles and Kenan much
earlier?" she asked.

Would he? When Cain was younger, he'd dreamed
about having brothers or sisters. Someone who would
be in the trenches with him. Maybe he wouldn't have
felt so alone or isolated. But as he'd grown up, he'd
stopped wishing for that. He wouldn't have wished his
existence with Barron on an enemy much less a sibling.

"Knowing about them now or ten years ago wouldn't
have changed anything," he said.

Maybe it'd been a blessing that he hadn't been aware
of them. They would've been just two more people his
father could've used against him. Like his mother.

"Barron had his own reasons for his actions. The
least of them being manipulation and power," he added,
then immediately cursed himself for revealing too
much. No way in hell was he getting into a discussion
about his hellish childhood with her.

With anyone.

"You can't mean that," she protested.

"About Barron? I damn well can."

"No." She shook her head. "About your brothers. I wish I had siblings. It would've meant someone who had your back. No matter what. No questions asked. It would've meant not being alone. What I wouldn't give to have that right now," she said softly.

So softly he had to wonder if she'd meant to voice the words aloud.

"Why are you alone, Devon? You might not have siblings, but what about family other than your father? You told me you came from a big family. What about them?"

She blinked. "You remember that?"

"I remember everything," he murmured.

About you. About that day.

He wished he didn't.

"Yes, I do have a large family. Between my father's and mother's sides, I have six aunts and four uncles. And a ton of cousins. I haven't seen them in years. Not since we moved from New Jersey."

Cain frowned. "New Jersey isn't across an ocean. It's not even five hours away. Why?"

Pain flickered in her eyes before her lashes lowered. But he caught the shadows it left.

"Initially, Dad's new firm demanded a lot of his time, so we didn't return to visit often. And then I guess everyone became busy because the phone calls slowed, then stopped, and we just lost touch." She shrugged a shoulder, but he didn't accept or believe the nonchalant gesture. Not for a minute. She missed that big Italian family she'd spoken of so affectionately in the garden.

And he suspected there was more to the story than she was admitting.

And he also suspected that "more" started and ended with Gregory Cole.

"Oh God." Her low exclamation refocused his attention on her and not on his darkening thoughts. "That's why you were in the garden the day of the funeral," she breathed, eyes widening. "Your father is who you were damning." Her full lips twisted. "Not only did you lose your father, but you discovered he'd been lying to you for years. No wonder you were furious. I'm so sorry. You should've been saying goodbye, grieving. Not having the rug pulled out from under you."

"You were my saving grace that day," he murmured.

He hadn't intended to let that slip, either. Even if it was the truth.

"Until I wasn't," she said, voice as soft.

"Until you weren't," he agreed. "But I'm still thankful. You reminded me of one very important fact. If it seems too good to be true, then it is," he drawled.

Satisfaction should've filled him at her barely concealed flinch. It didn't. He hadn't stated the obvious to hurt her so much as to drive home that she couldn't be trusted. Those pretty green eyes and that disarming honesty had tricked him once. Now that he'd made the mistake of kissing her, he was even more susceptible to disregarding what he knew about her and her father for another taste.

At this point, when his body was in danger of launching a full-out rebellion, he *needed* her to be the woman capable of deception and blackmail, and not the soft, desirable woman who'd welcomed his mouth and domination.

"I have a meeting I need to prepare for," he said, sliding his hands in his front pockets—and away from temptation.

If his blatant dismissal affected her, she didn't reveal it. Nodding, she crossed the room for the purse she'd deposited on the visitors chair before the photographer arrived. She stood for several seconds, staring at him, lips parted as if words hovered there. But, after a moment, she gave her head a shake and exited the office without glancing backward. The soft snick of the lock reverberated in the room.

And he was glad she wasn't there to witness his flinch.

Eight

I'm in hell.

Cain surveyed the large formal dining room full of people. It reminded him too damn much of his father's funeral. The guest list included business moguls, society darlings, celebrities and even a few professional athletes. Food and alcohol that probably cost more than most people's yearly salary. A beautiful decor including antiques and artwork that had probably netted some interior designer a mint. The laughter and chatter from jeweled, tuxedoed and gowned guests.

Except this time, instead of celebrating a death, they were toasting his engagement.

Same thing, in his opinion.

The only good part about this trip to purgatory was that Gregory Cole had insisted the party be held in his

Back Bay townhome instead of the mansion Cain had been forced to reside in for the next year. Any excuse he had to *not* spend time in that mausoleum, he grabbed.

Still, he had to hand it to Gregory. When the man threw a party, he didn't hold back. He'd gone all out to brag about his wealth and prowess to Boston society. Because regardless of what the invitations stated, this occasion wasn't about Cain and Devon. It was all about Gregory Cole. An opportunity to gather the very people he sought to impress in one place. This wasn't an engagement party but the beginning of his campaign to infiltrate their privileged, blue-blooded ranks. And like any good general, the man was a master strategist.

Disgust boiled inside Cain. He hated this. Hated the hypocrisy, the phoniness. And yet, here he stood, right in the midst of it, a hostage because of his loyalty to one person. The person he loved most in this world.

Emelia Farrell.

He scanned the room, and within seconds located his mother, as always, surrounded by a circle of admiring men and women. Though in her midfifties, in Cain's eyes, she hadn't aged a bit from the woman who'd read him bedtime stories when his father wasn't home to forbid her from coddling him. The woman who'd gifted him with his first camera on his twelfth birthday. The woman who'd yelled the loudest and longest when he'd graduated from both high school and college, when his father couldn't be bothered to attend either ceremony because of business trips. Time might've brushed her raven-black hair with touches of gray and grazed the corners of her eyes with lines, but it hadn't stooped the proud lines of her shoulders, hadn't dimmed the brightness of her blue eyes—or the love for him that shone there.

That love had brought her here tonight, to her ex-lover's home. Cain didn't know the details of her affair with Gregory, and he couldn't ask because she wasn't aware he possessed knowledge of it. Still, even if the relationship had ended amicably, Gregory now used it as a weapon against her and Cain. And damned if he would allow his mother to discover her affair with Gregory was the sword held to Cain's throat.

Unbidden, his focus shifted to the woman at his mother's side—his fiancée. Though his mother had met Devon for the first time tonight, she'd immediately taken to her. Even now, with their arms linked at the elbow, they appeared to be close friends instead of strangers who'd met only hours earlier. But how could his mother resist? Devon had assumed her friendly persona for the evening—the one that had snagged his attention. His mother had been enchanted and had told Cain so. Witnessing that delighted smile on her face—and the relief in her eyes—he hadn't possessed the heart to disappoint her by revealing Devon's true nature. How this engagement had more to do with mercenary greed rather than love.

As if sensing his perusal, Devon glanced away from the young man so animatedly talking to her and met Cain's gaze. Damn, those eyes. Capable of gleaming with amusement, then shadowed with sympathy and sadness, then glazing over with passion. Chameleon eyes. Gorgeous eyes. Secretive eyes.

Against his will, his attention dipped to her lush mouth, painted in a bold red that begged to be smeared. It called to him, just as her body did in a dark green, floor-length gown that should've been modest. But the material clinging to the high thrust of her breasts, the indent of her waist and the dramatic flare of her hips transformed the simple style into a billboard for a wet dream.

She was a princess holding court. Accepting all the attention and praise as her due. Regal and untouchable.

All lies.

Especially since he couldn't evict from his mind just how *touchable* she was.

"It's your engagement party, son." Gregory appeared beside him, clapping Cain on the shoulder. "You should be enjoying yourself instead of standing over here in the corner. Go mingle. After all, these people are here to celebrate you and your bride-to-be."

Cain snorted. At both the man and the admonishment. "These are *your* guests, not mine. And considering I was informed of this little get-together a couple of days ago when the invitations had been mailed out a week earlier, count yourself grateful I'm here at all." He shrugged off the other man's hand on the pretense of lifting his tumbler of Scotch to his mouth. "And don't ever call me son."

Gregory's smile tightened and anger flashed in his eyes. "You're not thinking of causing a scene in my home, are you, Cain? I wouldn't advise it." Tucking his hands into his front pockets, Gregory turned and made a show of surveying the room. "I was delighted that your mother chose to attend. She looks as beautiful as I remember."

Rage barreled through Cain, licking at the restraints binding his control. His vision flickered to crimson, and for a moment, real fear that he would hurt this man flashed through him.

"Listen to me, Cole," Cain growled, waiting for Gregory to swing his smug smile back to him before continuing, "and listen well. Don't comment on my mother. Don't look in her direction. Don't even fucking think about her. You believe you have me by the short hairs with your blackmail scheme, but if you upset her—if I even suspect you hurt her feelings or breathed in her direction—I will raze your world to the ground, and I don't give a damn if I go down in flames with you."

"You're in no position to threaten me," Gregory snapped.

"Threaten you? Oh no, Cole. It's a promise."

The older man glared at him, a muscle ticking along his jaw. "I—"

"There you are, Cain." Kenan strode up to them, Achilles beside him.

The two of them cut a wide path between the thick throng of people, leaving glances in their wake that ranged from admiring to curious to smirks and whispers. This was the first public appearance of the Farrell Bastards with their legitimate brother, after all. Irritation rose within him, swift and bright.

"Smart to position yourself near the bar," Achilles rumbled, stepping past Cain and requesting a beer from the bartender.

"The man might not be much of a talker, but when he does speak, he makes perfect sense," Kenan praised with a grin. He stretched a hand toward Gregory. "Kenan Rhodes. It's nice to meet Cain's future father-in-law."

"Yes," Gregory said, accepting his hand. "I've heard so much about you and your brother. Thank you for coming tonight."

"Of course." Kenan nodded, still smiling. He must've inherited that charm from his birth mother because God knew neither Cain nor Achilles had received it from their father. "Would you mind if we steal Cain from you for a moment?"

"Sure thing." Gregory cupped Cain's shoulder once more and squeezed. "We'll continue our talk later, Cain."

He didn't bother replying and as soon as the man disappeared into the crowd, Kenan snorted. "I just met the man, but he has me wanting to take a dip in a bleach bath." He slid Cain a glance. "No offense."

"None taken." Cain sipped his Scotch. "Believe me."

"Good thing you're marrying his daughter and not him," Achilles added, pushing off the small bar. "Although, I have to wonder if you're really marrying anyone."

Shock whipped through Cain. "What are you talking about?"

"Devon. Your fiancée," Achilles said, his deep voice lowering. "She wasn't wearing a ring during your engagement photo shoot. When a man proposes it's normally with a ring."

Shit. He forced himself not to look in Devon's direction. Or glance down at her bare fingers. He hadn't thought of buying her a ring—it hadn't occurred to him. His gut twisted. Who else had noticed? Were they speculating even now about why Cain Farrell hadn't bought his new fiancée—the woman he was supposed to be hopelessly in love with—an engagement ring?

"I don't think anyone else has noticed. Or at least they aren't gossiping about it," Kenan said.

"At least not within our hearing," Achilles muttered, tipping his bottle up for a sip.

"Anything you'd like to share?" Kenan asked, cocking his head to the side and studying Cain with a narrowed gaze.

The truth shoved at his throat, catching him by surprise. But he remained silent. Old habits died hard. He'd been the keeper of his family's secrets for so many years that he was a professional at not sharing his burdens with others. If he didn't hand over information to people, they couldn't use it against him.

They couldn't pity him.

Kenan sighed. "Listen, Cain, I'm well aware you don't think of us as brothers. And you haven't known us long enough to trust us. But you don't have to trust Achilles and me for us to have your back. Whatever you need us to say or do, just tell us. We don't need to know what's going on or why. Until you're ready to share."

It would've meant someone who had your back. No matter what. No questions asked. It would've meant not being alone.

Devon's wistful words drifted to him.

Kenan was right; he didn't trust them. Given his childhood, he'd learned at too young an age not to have unconditional faith in anyone except his mother. But here stood the two men who shared his DNA and not much else, offering him their loyalty? What had Cain done to earn that?

They were fools to give it.

And yet the words to say so froze on his tongue.

"Thanks," he said. Clearing his throat, he scanned the room for Devon. He spotted his mother but his "fiancée" no longer stood by her side. "Have either of you seen Devon?" he asked, frowning.

"No," Achilles said. "Last I saw, her father pulled her away from your mother to speak with her. That was several minutes ago." He arched an eyebrow. "Why? Is everything okay?"

Cain coerced his lips into a smile. "Of course. If you'll excuse me."

He laid his drink on the bar and went in search of Devon and Gregory. What was so important that Gregory would leave his guests to talk to Devon?

Unease slid between Cain's ribs, lodging in his chest. It couldn't mean anything good.

For him.

"Dad, what's going on? Is everything okay?" Devon frowned as she followed her father into the library.

Not that she was complaining about getting a breather from the party. No, she was thankful for the reprieve. These social events were tedious and painful for her at the best of times. But to be the center of attention? The focus of speculative glances and pseudo whispers? Many of which wondered how *she*, a fat nobody, had managed to snag one of the most eligible bachelors in the city.

Yes. Torture.

Her father, on the other hand, was in his element. Already, the fruits of his scheming labors were coming to pass with the who's who of Boston society. He was a king sitting on his throne. All he'd had to do was blackmail a man and sacrifice his daughter's future to accomplish it.

She studied her father as he strode to the built-in bar on the other side of the library and prepared a drink. She tried not to allow bitterness to swallow her whole. The man who'd taught her how to ride a bike and then tenderly picked her up and wiped her tears after she fell—he couldn't have entirely disappeared. The man her mother had loved still had to exist. And because of those memories and occasional glimpses of that loving, supportive father… Because of her mother and the promise Devon had made to her…she couldn't give up on him. She had to believe the man he'd been wasn't completely *lost*.

"How're you and Cain getting along?" he asked, his back to her.

She frowned. "Fine, I suppose." How did he expect them to get along? Cain was being blackmailed. He viewed her as one of the conspirators. He loathed her.

Even if he kisses like he filed the patent on it.

She mentally shook her head. As if lust had anything to do with affection or love. Donald had taught her that.

"Fine? You'll have to do better than that." He faced her, his drink in hand. "Do you think people haven't noticed that you two seem distant toward one another? This is your engagement party and neither of you appear happy to be here. People talk. Then they'll start to speculate." He swirled the amber alcohol in his glass. "You need to try harder, Devon. After everything I've arranged on your behalf, you need to do better so all of my hard work doesn't go to waste. This relationship might not have been his idea, but if you put in a little more effort, he may forget about that. I need Cain happy. And that is your responsibility."

"Careful, Dad," Devon drawled. "With talk like that, you're edging close to prostitution. And you're not pimping me out, are you?"

He uttered a sound somewhere between disgust and impatience. "Don't be ridiculous. This is all for you, for the children you'll one day have. So you will never have to endure what your mother and I did—poverty, powerlessness, invisibility. No one will look down on you, and I'm ensuring that. Is it pretty? No. But there's nothing fair about this world we live in. Even Cain understands that."

"I really think you believe that, Dad," she murmured, sadness hollowing out her chest. "But Mom would've been happy living in a Plainfield, New Jersey, duplex surrounded by family. And maybe we didn't live in a Back Bay townhome with money at our disposal, but we were happy. We had love, community and joy. We had each other. I don't care if other people accept me.

Money can't buy that acceptance and it definitely can't provide what we had back in Plainfield."

"Spoken like a person who has never known what it is to work their fingers to the bone to provide for their family," he sneered. "But that is in the past. Your mother isn't here, and I'm going to provide for you in the way I see fit. Which brings me to another topic…" He lifted his glass and sipped from it, regarding her from over the rim. "It's come to my attention that Farrell International has a real estate project in the works near TD Garden and North Station. It includes a concert venue, shops, an office tower, hotels, condominiums in a five-hundred-unit, sixty-floor residential tower, as well as transit upgrades to North Station. Farrell is apparently accepting only a handful of investors for the development. I intend to be one of those investors."

She shook her head, shrugging. "I don't know what that has to do with me."

"Everything," he countered. Placing his unfinished drink on the bar behind him, he strode across the room and halted in front of her. "Right now, Cain isn't feeling very…charitable toward me."

Devon snorted. Now wasn't *that* the understatement of the millennium.

"That's where you come in. I need you to convince him to invite me to be an investor on the project."

The crack of laughter escaped her before she could contain it. "You're not serious?" Another incredulous chuckle climbed the back of her throat but then she narrowed her gaze on her father's darkening expression. "You *are* serious," she whispered, stunned. "Dad, that's cra—"

"Thanks to me, you are now engaged to one of the most powerful men in Boston—"

"I didn't ask you to do that for me. I want nothing to do with it," she interrupted.

"Thanks to me, you are the envy of every woman in this house, in this city," he continued, raising his voice and rolling over her protest. "The very least you can do is help me. A project this size would mean millions in profit for not just me but for all of my clients. To be in business with Farrell International would establish my company as one of the wealthiest and most successful boutique investment firms in the country. All you have to do is speak to Cain and use your influence to convince him to let me in on it."

"Influence?" She scoffed, slicing a hand between them. "What influence? He hates me just a little bit less than he hates you. And even if I did have that kind of sway with him, I wouldn't do it. I have no idea what you're holding over him, but isn't it enough that you're forcing him into a marriage he wants no part of? Now you want to trick him into a business deal? No." She shook her head, vehement. "You were just telling me how all of this is for me. This is about you, Dad. All you. And I won't be a part of taking more from Cain."

"Where's your loyalty?" he snarled, crowding closer and jabbing a finger at her. "You are my daughter. Your first allegiance is to me, not to a man who wouldn't even know you existed if not for my hand pulling the strings. You owe me."

"I owe you?" she repeated on the tail end of a disbelieving chuckle. "And when do I stop paying, Dad? When is my bill wiped clean? When do I no longer need to whore myself out for your ambitions?"

Anger darkened his green eyes to nearly black pools and red mottled his skin. His mouth disappeared into a hard, angry line. He edged closer, looming over her. "Don't you ever talk to me like that—"

"Get the hell away from her."

Devon jolted. The seething fury in that voice had her jerking her head toward the library entrance. Her father stiffened, the corner of his mouth curling as he stepped back and turned to face Cain.

An avenging angel.

The words whispered through her head, and even though she acknowledged the sentiment as fanciful and silly, she couldn't erase it. With his powerful body, starkly beautiful face and an aura of righteous wrath, the only things missing were wings. She shivered. In apprehension? In fear? In...excitement? She didn't care to answer that question.

He stalked forward, and, oh God, part of her wanted to run to him, to burrow against that wide chest.

It was the need that kept her feet firmly rooted.

"This is family business, Cain," her father growled. "Which means it's none of yours."

"You made it my business when you forced your way into my life. When you threatened my mother's reputation. When you made your daughter collateral in a back-alley deal with my father. So no, Cole. Devon is my business."

Devon is my business.

The statement seemed to echo in the sudden stillness of the room. It reverberated in her ears like a pulse. Pounded in her chest like an anvil. Throbbed low in her belly like an ache. To a person who'd spent the last sixteen years of her life never belonging to anything, anyone or anywhere, that announcement hit her like a drug. One she would be wise to resist.

"This is ridiculous," her father bit out. "I have guests."

Throwing one more glare at her, he stormed out of the library, the door closing with a heavy click. Silence vibrated in the room, so dense, she swore it pressed against her skin. Anger still clung to Cain, but it didn't alarm or frighten her. His outrage was on her behalf, not directed at her.

When was the last time someone had leaped to her defense? Had sought to protect instead of use her? For the second time in as many minutes, she shied away from answers she would regret.

"Has he ever put his hands on you?" Cain ground out, his predator eyes blazing bright.

"No," she whispered. Then clearing her throat, she shook her head for added emphasis. "No, he wouldn't do that. Whatever your opinion of him, he's never been physically abusive."

Being emotionally neglectful was another matter.

"You're not lying to me, are you, Devon?" he pressed, his gaze searching her face. She fought not to squirm under its inspection. "You're not just trying to protect him?"

Irritation surged within her, but something—call it intuition—suppressed the flash of impatience. Beneath the rigid lines of his face and the growl in his voice lurked...worry? No. It was deeper than that. More... visceral. It was darker. Her heart knocked against her sternum as a completely absurd thought crept into her head, twisted her belly.

Had Barron Farrell hurt Cain?

As soon as the thought flickered through her mind, she slapped it down. Impossible. God no. She had no proof of that whatsoever. In an insular ecosystem such as Boston society, surely she would've heard some kind of rumor.

You just don't want to imagine it's possible.

An image of a younger Cain shrinking away from a larger, malevolent figure shot inside her head before she could stop it. Cain in pain, scared, victimized... She clenched her fingers into fists, the sudden, fierce longing to strike out against that figure so strong, so intense, a tremble shivered through her.

But in the next instant, she silently ordered herself to calm down, to get it together. Cain had walked in on an argument between her and her father. Yes, his assumption had been wrong, but objectively she could understand why he'd come to that conclusion. None of that meant he was a victim of abuse himself.

Given her overactive imagination, maybe she needed to start writing fantasy novels.

"No, I'm not covering for him," she finally replied. "Cain, I promise you. I wouldn't lie to you about that."

He stared at her for several more moments before nodding, the movement stiff.

"What were you arguing about?" he demanded.

The truth pushed at her throat, but that loyalty her father accused her of not having shoved back. If she told Cain about her father's request, he would see it as another attempt to manipulate him, to extort him. Gregory held something over Cain, but the billionaire reminded her of a prowling beast, waiting for just the right opening to leap and devour. She refused to be the conduit for that opportunity. Gregory might not value prudence when it came to this man, but she did. And if she had to save her father from himself, then so be it.

But speaking of the something Gregory held over Cain…

She moved toward him even though every primal instinct shouted she should maintain a safe distance. Still, she didn't stop until only inches separated them, and she had to tilt her head back to peer up into his face. His earthy, woodsy scent filled her nose. His heat called out to her, enticed her to share it. Briefly, she closed her eyes, combatting the lure that was *him*.

"You said my father threatened your mother's reputation. What did you mean?" she asked, fairly certain he wouldn't grant her the truth. Since he believed her to be her father's accomplice, he probably assumed she knew and was engaging in a coy game.

He didn't reply, but stared down at her, ice chilling his eyes. She read the "fuck you" there before he uttered it.

But he didn't utter it.

"Your father and my mother had an affair several years ago. My parents' marriage was not a happy one. Since I was old enough to understand what their arguments meant, I knew Barron was unfaithful. When your father arrived at my office to tell me about the affair, I didn't judge her. She just made the mistake of having an affair with the wrong man."

He calls his father by his first name.

The words swirled in her head.

"Apparently, before Barron died, Gregory went to him with evidence of his affair with Mom. Videos, pictures, texts, emails. To keep it from going public, no doubt so he didn't look like a fool who couldn't satisfy his wife," Cain sneered, disgust dripping from his tone, "Barron signed a contract with your father. The terms were simple—Gregory remained quiet about the affair and agreed not to release any of his evidence to the press and my father would hand me over."

Oh God. She splayed her hand over her rapidly pounding heart. There was only one place for this to head. One. And part of her couldn't stand to hear it. The filthy by association part.

"The week after Barron's funeral, your father showed up with his contract, demanding I honor it, or he would ensure every trash tabloid and gossip site received those pictures, videos and texts. I either marry his daughter or sit by and watch my mother's reputation be ripped apart click by click, view by view. So, I agreed."

She gasped—disbelief, repulsion and pain struck her like tiny fists. White noise exploded in her head and bile scorched a path toward her throat. How could her father do that? How could he use Cain's *mother* as a bargaining chip? Would he have been so quick to do the same to her own mother? To his wife? Where did his boundaries lie? Or had greed and ambition obliterated all lines?

She was going to be sick. Her suddenly leaden feet stumbled back. She clutched a hand to her stomach, bending over at the waist.

Out of the corner of her eye, she caught Cain's movement toward her, but she shot out an arm, palm up in the age-old signal of stop. She couldn't bear a touch. Not when she was so fragile. One gentle wisp of air would shatter her.

But he didn't stop. He walked around her, and strong, muscular arms encircled her from behind, steadying her, holding her up when her legs threatened to give out. A rock-hard chest braced her while powerful thighs supported her. All that strength and brawn—for her, and she greedily, shamelessly, took advantage.

By sheer force of will, she swallowed and held off the overwhelming surge of nausea. But the effort left her trembling, shaking.

"I didn't know," she rasped, voice hoarse from the silent sobs that had torn at her throat. "I swear, I didn't know."

No wonder he hated her; in his eyes, she was complicit in the vile threat against his mother. To him, she was the selfish bitch who used any means necessary to marry a man for his connections. He couldn't know she was as much a hostage to her father's schemes as he was—and she couldn't tell him.

But would it even matter? She was the daughter of the man who was blackmailing him. She was stealing his future with a woman he could truly love.

"Easy, sweetheart. Just breathe. Follow me." He bent his head over hers, his mouth brushing her cheek. "In and out. In. And out." He inhaled and exhaled several slow, deep breaths. Without a conscious decision, she followed his lead. In. Out. In. Out. Eventually, her tempo matched his, and she calmed, relaxing back against him.

Only their breathing punctuated the air. Seconds passed into minutes. And at some point, as the back of her head rested against his collarbone, the cyclone of pain, anger and disillusionment segued into another kind of storm. One where she became aware of the carefully leashed power in the arm wrapped around her, just under her breasts.

One where she noticed how his long, hard legs surrounded hers. Where she noted how his chest rose and fell on a slightly faster rhythm, matching the hot blasts of air that grazed Devon's cheek.

Where the steely length of his cock nudged the rise of her behind and small of her back.

Where she fought not to arch and rub against that length. Fought and failed.

Tempting the beast was an act of lunacy. And yet, as his low rumble vibrated in her ear and against her back, she couldn't bring herself to give a damn.

The arm around her tightened and his free hand caressed her shoulder before trailing over her collarbone and then necklacing her throat. She gasped under the weight of that big palm and those long fingers, a thrill spiraling through her at the heaviness of his hold—at the possessiveness. He didn't squeeze, but he didn't have to. Soft pants broke on her lips as the flesh between her legs swelled, moistened, pulsed.

Like prey, she arched her neck, exposing her throat to him. Exposing her vulnerability to him.

Her lashes lifted and her eyes clashed with his sharp wolf's gaze. Unmistakable lust burned bright and the hunger there stoked the needy flames leaping and dancing inside her. And when he leaned his head down, she tipped her head back farther, rising on her tiptoes to meet the carnal beauty of his mouth.

Unlike the kiss during the engagement shoot, this one lacked gentleness. It was fury. Wild. Raw. So wet. A clashing of tongues, teeth and wills. Though she'd surrendered, she was not meek.

With a lick against the roof of his mouth, she dared him to duel with her. With a thrust and slide of her tongue she ordered him to give her more. With a hard suck she showed him she could take all that he dished out. That she *wanted* to take it.

His long fingers splayed higher on her throat, tilting her head to the side so he could dive deeper, claim all of her. She opened wider, offered him…everything.

She lifted an arm, grabbed the nape of his neck even as she arched like a tightly strung bow and rubbed over the thick column of flesh branding her. In answer, his grip tightened a fraction and his hips ground into her, enflaming the hot, grasping need inside her. She whimpered into his mouth, and he swallowed it, exchanging it for a groan.

The arm banding her torso loosened, but before she could object, his hand cupped her breast, molding it, plumping it. The material of her dress proved an inadequate barrier to his bold, questing fingers, and when he pinched her nipple, the electrical current jolted from her breasts to her sex. Her whimper morphed into a cry. But not one of pain. *God no*. One of pleasure. So much pleasure. Almost too much. How was that possible? His thumb swept across the tip, circling, then tweaking. And as another bolt of ecstasy ripped through her, she didn't care about the logistics of how and why. Just that he. Didn't. Stop.

"Cain," she gasped against his lips. "Please."

He stiffened behind her, his hands on her, freezing. Silently, a wail of protest screamed in her head, momentarily deafening her. And she wanted to demand—hell, beg—that he continue what he'd started. To not leave her aching. Hurting.

But as if his name on her tongue had shattered their sensual haze, he snatched his arms away, leaving her adrift, confused by the sudden lack of contact. She shuddered, the cool air of the room reaching her now that the furnace of his body no longer surrounded her. In defense—in self-protection—she wrapped her arms around herself.

"That shouldn't have happened," he rumbled from behind her, and the words struck her like an icy blow. She should've expected his regret; she was the enemy, and unlike the engagement photo shoot, there were no witnesses here to convince. Of course, he wouldn't be thrilled about kissing her, touching her. And yet... A wounded throb pounded inside her chest, her stomach.

What was it about her that made it so hard for others to want her? Made it so easy for them to reject her? To leave?

A sob lodged itself in the base of her throat, but she refused it passage. With that kiss, she might have betrayed her attraction to him, but damn if she would hand over her pride, too. If he could be unaffected, so could she.

So *would* she.

Schooling her expression into an aloof mask, she turned to face him.

"A mistake on both our parts," she said, proud how her voice didn't reflect the pain that still trembled inside her. "We'll both make sure there's not a repeat performance," she added, beating him to the "this can't happen again" speech.

Cain stared at her, and she couldn't keep her gaze from dipping to his swollen, damp mouth. Swollen and damp from her kiss. Despite the hurt pumping through her veins, lust stirred low in her belly. Dammit. She knew not to invest more into a relationship than the other person. That deficit had nearly destroyed her confidence, trampled her pride, battered her heart.

Texans remembered the Alamo. She remembered Donald.

Desire didn't equal affection. Didn't even equal *like*. And as hard as Cain's dick had been when pressed against her, he didn't care for her. Quite the contrary. If

Get Up To 4 Free Books!

Dear Reader,

IT'S A FACT: if you answer 4 quick questions, we'll send you 4 FREE REWARDS from each series you try!

Try **Harlequin® Desire** books featuring the worlds of the American elite with juicy plot twists, delicious sensuality and intriguing scandal.

Try **Harlequin Presents®** Larger-Print books featuring the glamourous lives of royals and billionaires in a world of exotic locations, where passion knows no bounds.

Or **TRY BOTH!**

I'm not kidding you. As a leading publisher of women's fiction, we value your opinions... and your time. That's why we are prepared to reward you handsomely for completing our mini-survey. In fact, we have 4 Free Rewards for you, including 2 free books and 2 free gifts from each series you try!

Thank you for participating in our survey,

Pam Powers

To get your 4 FREE REWARDS:
Complete the survey below and return the insert today to receive up to 4 FREE BOOKS and FREE GIFTS guaranteed!

"4 for 4" MINI-SURVEY

1 Is reading one of your favorite hobbies?

☐ YES ☐ NO

2 Do you prefer to read instead of watch TV?

☐ YES ☐ NO

3 Do you read newspapers and magazines?

☐ YES ☐ NO

4 Do you enjoy trying new book series with FREE BOOKS?

☐ YES ☐ NO

Please send me my Free Rewards, consisting of **2 Free Books from each series I select** and **Free Mystery Gifts**. I understand that I am under no obligation to buy anything, as explained on the back of this card.

☐ **Harlequin Desire®** (225/326 HDL GQ3X)
☐ **Harlequin Presents® Larger-Print** (176/376 HDL GQ3X)
☐ **Try Both** (225/326 & 176/376 HDL GQ4A)

FIRST NAME | LAST NAME

ADDRESS

APT.# | CITY

STATE/PROV. | ZIP/POSTAL CODE

EMAIL ☐ Please check this box if you would like to receive newsletters and promotional emails from Harlequin Enterprises ULC and its affiliates. You can unsubscribe anytime.

HD/HP-520-MS20

HARLEQUIN READER SERVICE—Here's how it works:

he had a choice—if her father granted him the choice—he would want nothing to do with her.

"Is that what that was? A performance?" he asked, and the rough texture of his tone rasped over her skin. "With no audience?"

"You're here, an audience of one. Besides, what else would it be? You're the one who told me to make my supposed love for you believable," she lied. "Consider that a dry run." She smiled, and it felt brittle and stiff. "We should return to the party. Any longer and people will wonder where we are."

But he didn't move. Just continued to study her in a way that threatened to carve away her emotional shield facade by facade, lie by lie.

"Right, we can't allow people to start gossiping about us," he drawled. "But do me one favor." He stepped forward and pressed his hard chest and thighs to hers, and his erection... She locked down the moan that rose within. His erection, still hard, still insistent, prodded her belly. Pride refused to let her shift backward. Refused to let him see how his aroused flesh had need clawing at her.

Before she could ask about the favor, he brushed his thumb across her bottom lip. Once, twice before pushing down on it.

"Don't replace your lipstick. One look at this swollen mouth and people will know I fucked it. That, too, is good for the validity of the performance."

His callous words had a dual effect—they angered her...and they had her sex tightening so hard, she squeezed her thighs against the erotic pull.

He dropped his hand and stepped back, placing distance between them. "After you," he mocked, sweeping an arm toward the library entrance. "We don't want to keep the masses waiting."

She ordered her legs to move, and thankfully, they followed her command. Not glancing at Cain, she strode toward the door, deliberately keeping her pace steady and casual.

Priority number one. Get through this farce of a party.

Priority number one-point-five. Patching up her defenses against Cain. That kiss had shaken them like boulders catapulted against stone barricades.

Because if she didn't, the consequences terrified her.

Not that he would get in.

But what she would let escape.

Her heart.

Nine

Cain pulled into a parking spot in front of the East Boston community center. Frowning, he nabbed his cell from the dashboard console and brought up Devon's text. He glanced at the address, then shifted his gaze to the GPS dash. Yes, it was the correct address.

Shutting off the engine of his Lexus RX 350, he exited the vehicle and surveyed the large red brick building set in the middle of the residential block. A couple of apartment buildings rose behind it and a city park sat across the street. A fenced-in playground, a couple of basketball courts and a paved lot painted blue with hopscotch blocks and a four-square game fanned out from the center. With it being well after dusk, no kids climbed the jungle gym. From the equipment that appeared old but well tended, the care and pride the administrators took in the center was apparent.

Still… Why did Devon ask him to meet her here? Was this a pet project and she intended to hit him up for a donation? At least the avarice would be for a good cause. He couldn't really fault her. When it came to obtaining funds for the charities she supported, his mother had been known to be rather cutthroat as well.

He held up his wrist and peered down at his watch. A little after six. If they were going to be on time for this dinner party her father was hosting—one Cain was attending only because several businessmen he knew were also going to be present—then they had to leave in the next twenty minutes. Which meant her pitch would have to wait for another time.

He approached the entrance to the building and, pulling the door open, stepped into the lobby. A semicircular desk manned by a security guard claimed one corner and a couple of tables cluttered with brochures took up another. A large corkboard took up one wall and artwork that ranged from childlike to more mature drawings covered it. The effect was professional yet welcoming. And warm. He could see only a corridor past the security desk, but the muffled sounds of voices and laughter echoed from that direction. There was happiness here, and safety.

"Can I help you, sir?" the older guard asked as Cain neared the desk.

"Yes, I'm here for Devon Cole. She's expecting me."

A smile brightened his face, as if just the mention of her name brought him pleasure. "Yes." He lifted a sign-in book and set it on the desktop. "You must be Mr. Farrell. Devon let me know you would be stopping by. Please log in your name and the time, and here's your visitor's badge." He slid a laminated card with a silver clip attached toward Cain.

After he finished entering his information and picked up the badge, the guard smiled once more. "She's in classroom number seven. Take this corridor to the end, go up the stairs and it's the last room on the right."

"Thank you." He nodded and started down the hall.

A sliver of anticipation slid through him, and he resented the hell out of it. But he couldn't deny it. It'd been a couple of weeks since the sham engagement party—and that incendiary kiss in the library. A couple of weeks since his body had been his own. Every night he went to bed, she owned him. Because it was images of her in his mind as he stroked himself.

They'd made several public appearances since then, and each time he had to circle her waist, hold her to his side, pretend to be one half of an adoring couple. It was torture. That probably made him a masochist because every hit of her honey-and-citrus scent, every brush of her hip, every glance at that wicked mouth... Yeah, torture of the sweetest, dirtiest kind.

And yet, he held back. Didn't even try to cross the line they'd crossed that night. Finding her with her father—with Gregory looming over her like the bully Cain knew him to be—had triggered Cain. His memories. Those age-worn but still sensitive feelings of rage, helplessness, fear. Her assurances that Gregory had never physically abused her had mollified the anger, but comforting her, holding her, had transmuted the emotion to a ravenous need that incinerated his control. Burned through him with the speed and destruction of a forest fire.

God, she'd been sweet. And potent. And lethal to his resolve. To his vow never to be under the thumb of another person. To never be *weak*.

Devon might not have known what her father had used as a threat—he believed her about that; her reaction had been too real, too visceral—but lack of knowledge about the details didn't absolve her of responsibility. She was still a willing participant in her father's blackmail. Like he'd told her weeks ago, she could refuse to participate and the scheme would end. But she didn't. And so, giving in to the undeniable desire between them—her hungry mouth and taut nipples hadn't lied about that desire—would be akin to capitulating to manipulation. To once more submit to someone else's control, when he'd promised himself it would never happen again.

He would never be powerless again.

Barron Farrell had taught him early on that love was a convenient excuse to cuff another person's will, to strangle their individual and emotional freedom…to steal their choices.

Cain wanted no part of the promise of pleasure in Devon's eyes or the vulnerability she stirred in him.

The rise of voices behind a closed door dragged him from his thoughts, and he zeroed in on the number above it: 7. He grabbed the knob, and after a brief pause, twisted it and pulled the door open.

Desks that wouldn't have been out of place in a high school were arranged on either side of the classroom and Devon stood in the middle aisle. Neither she nor the kids—ranging from early teens to young adults—noticed him standing just inside the entrance. One half of the room celebrated with high fives and fist bumps while the other side groaned and yelled good-natured gibes.

"Okay, okay," Devon said, pushing her hands down in a "shush" motion. "Team Come At Me Bro, this is your chance to tie the score. Answer this question correctly or Team It's About to Go Down will be ahead by three hundred points." The kids quieted, and she faced the catcalling side. "Ready?" She held up a white card. "For three hundred points in the category of music. What is the name of the most famous left-handed guitarist?"

That's easy, Cain silently scoffed. *Jimi Hendrix.*

But the teens didn't immediately shout out the answer. They huddled together, furiously whispering. Then a young girl wearing a Hobbits Run Middle Earth T-shirt and beautiful dreads leaned in and murmured something to her team with an adamant wave of her hand. The other kids glanced at each other and shrugged.

Turning to Devon, the girl stood and stated loudly, "Jimi Hendrix."

Devon stared at her, letting a dramatic pause fall over the room. "You're correct."

Stunned, Cain found himself smiling and mentally cheering with the team as they broke out in loud victorious shouts and some kind of dancing that looked both jerky and coordinated.

His bark of laughter took both him and the others by

surprise. The room fell silent as all eyes swung his way. For the first time in years, a bout of self-consciousness swelled inside him, but he met the thirty or so gazes fixed on him. One thing he remembered from high school—never show weakness. Thankfully, curiosity and surprise filled their stares instead of the calculation and pettiness he recalled from his younger years at the exclusive prep school Barron had insisted his son attend.

"Cain," Devon greeted, and then reached behind her to remove a cell phone from the pocket of her entirely-too-tight-for-his-sanity skinny jeans. Peeking down at the screen, she winced. "I'm sorry, I lost track of time. We were just finishing up here..."

"Uh-uh," a tall, blond boy from the opposing side objected. "We still have two more rounds to go. You can't just quit in the middle of Trivia Titans! This is war! And there's a pizza party at stake!"

Cain smothered a snort at the exaggerated protest and the outrage coloring the kid's declaration of battle.

Devon glanced at him, uncertainty flickering in her eyes. "Could you give me a few minutes to finish up here?"

"Yes." And then, before he could ask himself, "What the hell?" he shrugged out of his suit jacket and laid it across an empty desk. "Which team should I join?"

Shock widened her eyes and parted her pretty lips. With effort, he dragged his inspection from how soft and giving he knew that mouth to be and arrowed in on the team that included the *Lord of the Rings* fan. "Do you mind?" he prompted.

The teens stared at him in disbelief, some of them

surveying his white shirt, blue-and-gray-striped tie, black dress pants and shoes. But in the next moment, almost to a person, they broke out in grins. "Hell no!" one boy yelled, waving him over.

"Justin," Devon reprimanded with a frown.

The boy shrugged, offering her a sheepish smile. "My bad, Ms. Cole. I mean, yes, sir. Please do join us." He threw the overdone invitation at Cain, who didn't bother to contain his chuckle.

Cain slid into a desk next to Justin, and a series of objections and boos rose from the other side.

"No fair," a younger teen girl yelled, eyes narrowed behind her bright blue eyeglass frames. "That means you have to play for us, Ms. Cole."

"I can't—"

"No problem, Ms. C," another student rose from Cain's team, her hand outstretched to Devon. "I'll take over the questions. Besides," she curled her lip in a mock sneer directed at the opposing side, "they need all the help they can get."

The noise level in the room rose to deafening as everyone started tossing out smack talk. In a couple of minutes, though, Devon had confiscated a desk across from Cain's adopted team and the trivia battle resumed.

"All right, Team It's About to Go Down. For two hundred points… In the category of sports. Who ran the world's first marathon?"

They answered correctly with Philippides, and the next forty-five minutes passed in a furious and often hilarious blur of questions, answers, cheers, taunts and laughter. As the *Lord of the Rings* fan, whose name he'd learned was DeAndrea, emitted a battle cry that would've made William Wallace envious, Cain realized with more than a little astonishment that he was having fun.

When was the last time he'd just enjoyed himself? When he laughed, relaxed and let go of the weight that had burdened his shoulders since—well, a long damn time.

It felt…good.

He glanced at Devon, who was clustered with her team, preparing for the next question. The kids gathered around her, throwing their arms around her shoulders with affection. They obviously loved her. Trusted her. What did they know that he didn't? This side of her—openly friendly and caring and funny—he hadn't glimpsed it since the garden. Not surprising given their recent history. But she gave that to these kids without reservation.

And Cain wanted it again. Craved it.

As if she sensed his regard, she lifted her head and met his gaze. Emerald eyes lit with humor. Pink flushing her cheekbones. Sensual lips curved in an easy smile. Thick hair that he dreamed of having tangled around him pulled back into a high ponytail.

She was beautiful.

Who was the real Devon Cole? This playful, warm woman? The manipulative, grasping social climber? The hurt daughter, horrified to the point of sickness at her father's actions? The passionate, greedy lover who'd burned in his arms?

"Hey, cut it out!" the girl with the blue glasses

shouted, jabbing a finger in his direction. "No sending Ms. Cole the kissy eyes. You're the enemy!"

Devon's face flamed, and Cain grinned at her obvious embarrassment.

"That's her man, he can do whatever he wants," DeAndrea countered. "And all's fair in love and war."

It was official. The girl not only had fantastic taste in fiction, she was now his best friend and ally.

Laughter exploded from the back of the room. At some point, a crowd of kids and adults had crowded in to witness the competition.

Ten minutes later, Trivia Titans ended with Team Come At Me Bro, Cain's team, beating out Team It's About to Go Down by one hundred points. He waited until the cheers and yells had died down before lifting his hands.

"In thanks for letting me join in and for Ms. Cole for inviting me down here, I'm treating everyone to a pizza party. The entire community center."

The kids who hadn't participated in the competition jumped to their feet, adding their shouts to the others. Several more minutes passed before Devon calmed them down and instructed them to meet their parents downstairs or get ready for the center's van to carry them home.

As the kids filed out, they clapped their hands to his in high fives or bumped fists with him. A few hugged him, and his chest tightened at all the signs of acceptance.

When the door closed behind the last child, Devon turned to him, her hands clasped in front of her. The smile she'd worn for the last hour remained, but no longer reached her shuttered gaze. He instantly regretted the loss of that friendly, unguarded grin.

"Thank you for the pizza party, Cain. You didn't have to do that." She shook her head as she set about straightening the desks. "And I don't think you realize what you signed up for. Those kids can *eat*." She chuckled.

"I remember the hollow leg I had at that age. Especially for pizza. But no need to thank me. It's the least I can do for the fun they gave me this evening. It's… been a while," he murmured, crossing the room and helping her rearrange the desks.

"What's 'a while'?" she asked.

He paused, glancing over at her, but she continued with her task, not meeting his eyes. Used to keeping his own council for so long, the words lodged in his throat. But, straightening, he waited until she paused as well and turned, locking gazes with him.

"Longer than I can remember," he murmured.

She studied him, her scrutiny almost uncomfortable.

"I'm sorry for that, Cain," she said, and he restrained his instinctive flinch at the compassion in her voice. "But I'm glad you could find it here. That the kids could give those moments to you."

Not just the kids.

He locked down the words, but he couldn't deny the truth of them.

Turning away from her—and himself—he resumed straightening the desks. But he couldn't suppress his curiosity about her. About this side of her.

"When I walked in here, I expected you to pitch for a donation, not be the host to a trivia throwdown. Most women I know focus their energy on raising funds for an organization or sitting on its board, not getting their hands dirty. What are you doing here, Devon?"

"I work here."

He paused, surprise shooting through him. "Volunteer, you mean?"

A ghost of a smile teased the corner of her mouth before she shook her head. "No, I mean I work here. Draw a paycheck. I'm the youth coordinator for the community center."

Giving her his complete attention, he crossed his arms over his chest and frowned. "Why?"

"Why do I work here? Because this place is important to the community. It provides not only after-school care, but much needed services for children and senior citizens. The center is a safe place—"

"No." He waved his hand through the air. "Why do you need to work here? You can't convince me Gregory doesn't provide for his own daughter."

"I don't need to—well, I take that back. Yes, I do. This is where I belong, where I'm useful and have a purpose. These kids don't just need me, I need them, too. But a paycheck isn't just about money. It's insurance, security and stability. It's independence. I earned this job on my own merit, and no one can take it away from me." A shadow passed over her face, momentarily darkening her eyes. "At least not without a fight."

"What are you saying?" he asked, unease and suspicion crowding into his mind. "Has your father threatened not to support you? To kick you out? To get you fired?"

Gregory Cole had gone to extreme and illegal lengths to obtain an advantageous match for his daughter. He knew the man had no moral compass.

She shrugged a shoulder and gave a short shake of her head before striding over to the large desk in the front of the room. "Everyone's capable of anything under the right circumstance," she tossed out, her voice nonchalant. But the tension transforming her normally graceful movements into stiff ones belied that tone.

What did that mean? Was she referring to her father... or him? Guilt swarmed inside him, buzzing, stinging.

But dammit, they weren't friends. Weren't allies.

The battle lines had been drawn between them when she and her father had extorted him. For the last few weeks, he'd been fighting for autonomy over his professional and personal life. No one had ever accused him of fighting dirty, but when it came to never again being that powerless boy, he would get down in the mud and roll around in it.

Yet, the urge to pull her into his arms, to comfort her, to apologize, lingered like a grimy aftertaste.

"Who are you, Devon?" he murmured, the question out before he realized it had even formed in his head.

But he didn't rescind it.

She stared at him, her expressive eyes unreadable. Then that same small smile, this one containing a touch of wistfulness, teased her mouth before dropping away. "You don't really want to know the answer to that, Cain," she replied softly.

Before he could demand clarification, she pulled open the desk drawer and removed her purse. "My dress is in my office. Just give me twenty minutes to change, and I'll be ready to go."

He nodded, quiet as he followed her from the classroom.

This woman was an enigma. A beautiful, seductive enigma. And while he'd always loved to solve puzzles, she was one he would be better off leaving a mystery.

Ten

Devon glanced at the ornate clock mounted on the foyer wall.

6:28.

Cain should be arriving any moment for another night out—another performance as the loving, happily engaged couple. Cupping her left hand, she brushed her fingertips over the gorgeous four-carat, princess cut diamond ring encircling her finger. Any woman would be delighted to receive it—including her. Not ostentatious, but elegant, with small, flower-shaped emeralds decorating the band and adding a touch of whimsy. Oh yes, it was a dream ring, and she would be a liar if she claimed the sight of it hadn't squeezed her heart.

But in the next moment, a deep sadness had filled her.

Because the ring was a lie.

Another lie in a chain of them that slowly strangled her more and more each day. And each time she slipped it on her finger, the weight of it became heavier and heavier. A constant reminder that she was so enmeshed in this sordid mess that her father had created, she couldn't inhale a breath that didn't contain the acrid, bitter tang of deception.

And ever since Cain had visited the community center two weeks ago and revealed the man who existed beneath the cold, embittered executive, the act had become even harder to perpetrate. The truth had become more difficult to confine.

When he'd asked her who she really was… Her throat had ached with restraining a plea for him to see her. Take a hard look past his preconceptions and really *see* her. The need to inform him that he wasn't the only victim of her father's blackmail clawed at her. But she'd glanced around the empty classroom, envisioned how it'd appeared only minutes earlier, packed with excited kids safe from the dangerous lures of the streets, learning and having a ball.

And she'd remained silent.

Because confessing to Cain would've been for her sake alone. Being quiet was for the teens she loved, the staff who devoted their time and hearts, the community who depended on the center's existence.

So she continued to play her role. Continued to participate in this charade of a romance that at times careened too dangerously close to feeling real.

She wouldn't emerge from this unscathed. And that

terrified her almost as much as losing the community center.

Her left hand curled into a fist, the lights from the foyer's chandelier bouncing off the diamond.

Oh yes. Beautiful lies.

The doorbell chimed, snatching her from her morose thoughts. Swiping her damp palms down her thighs, she moved forward and unlocked the door. She didn't need to glance through the video monitor; she expected only one person this evening.

Pulling open the door, she revealed Cain standing on the other side. His bright gaze met hers before dipping to the black high-waisted cocktail dress with the daring square neckline and roaming down to the stilettos with a delicate ankle strap. When his regard returned to her face, she sucked in a low breath at the heat flickering in those beautiful depths. The same warmth tingled her skin, swirled low in her belly…instigated a sweet, acute ache between her legs.

Her body had no shame when it came to this man.

And he hadn't even touched her.

Yet.

Her body already braced itself for the solicitous presses of his hand to the small of her back, the sensual cupping of the nape of her neck, the possessive curl of his arm around her waist. By the time he returned her home after these little outings, she resembled a noodle—wet and damn near limp with desire.

If she didn't know for a fact that the man despised her, she would accuse him of diabolically torturing her with the sex he exuded like a pheromone.

"You look beautiful," Cain said, the deep inflection a rough caress over her skin.

It wasn't the first time he'd complimented her, but it never failed to leave her flustered and a bit disbelieving. Cain might not possess the reputation of a playboy, but previous to their "engagement," he had been caught by photographers with women on his arm. Women who looked nothing like her. Tall, slender, sophisticated, worldly.

Not short, full-figured, a little naive. Especially when it came to this world he navigated with the precision and skill of a shark piloting through dark, predator-infested waters. She harbored zero doubts that if her father hadn't manipulated and schemed, that meeting in Cain's garden would've been their first and last. He wouldn't have sought her out. Wouldn't have kissed her as if she had become his air, food and shelter—everything he needed to survive.

More lies.

"Thank you," she murmured, turning and picking up the coat she'd tossed over the chair. Before she could slide into it, Cain stepped forward and gently but firmly took the garment from her. He held it up, and she slipped her arms through the sleeves. "Thanks," she repeated, tying the belt. "I'm ready."

Nodding, he grasped her elbow and steered her out of the house. Minutes later, they pulled away from the curb and joined Back Bay's Saturday night traffic. She stared out the window, lost in her thoughts, but soon realized they were headed in the opposite direction of downtown and the reception for the gallery opening.

Her father had issued the invitation as one of his clients owned the art gallery. In other words, he wanted to flaunt his association with Cain like a national flag.

"Cain, unless this is an unusual shortcut, this isn't the way to the reception."

He glanced over at her, his gaze hooded. "We're skipping it."

She blinked. Stared at him. Or his sharp profile since he'd returned his attention to the road. "But…" she stuttered.

Oh, Dad isn't going to like this.

As if he read her mind, Cain stated, "I told your father once before that just because he barks doesn't mean I heel. I've attended several of the other events because they were beneficial to me. Tonight, he intends to prance me around the room like a show pony, and I'm not anyone's stud. Besides," he added, shooting another undecipherable look in her direction. "I made other plans."

She didn't ask what those plans were.

Jesus, his refusal to kowtow to her father shouldn't be so damn *hot*. No man of her acquaintance had ever dared to defy Gregory Cole. Quite the opposite—they catered to him. Donald had pursued her just to get to her father. But Cain's attitude? She would never have to worry if Gregory's appeal was stronger than hers. Never have to fear his ulterior motives.

Ludicrous given their circumstances, but there was something…freeing in that knowledge. Freeing and just damn *hot*.

By the time she got herself together, Cain arrived at

a home—if one could call a stately, historic mansion a home—she recognized.

"Your house?" She tore her gaze from the monolith of old Beacon Hill wealth to throw a confused glance at Cain. But he didn't answer her. He shoved open his car door and rounded the hood to open hers. "Cain?" she pressed, sliding her palm across the one he extended toward her.

"Dinner, Devon," he replied, drawing her from the vehicle and shutting the door behind her. "Trust me."

Oh God no.

She realized the comment had been offhand, but it resounded in her head.

She wasn't that far gone. To trust him would be to make herself vulnerable to him, and that would never happen.

As he guided her past the iron gate and up the walk and front steps, the cold, intimidating grandness of the place struck her again as it had the day of Barron Farrell's funeral. White stone with large bay windows, lit sconces and turrets that reminded her of a castle, the postcolonial mansion overlooked the Public Garden like a silent sentinel.

"I can't believe you grew up here," she breathed. Yes, she sounded like an awed tourist, but so what. It wasn't every day a person encountered something straight out of *Game of Thrones.* "This house is…wow. I heard someone mention—" okay, so it'd been her father "—that it's been in your family for generations."

"Yes, four generations of Farrells have dwelled in these hallowed halls," he said, his voice so flat, so…

careful around the obviously mocking words, that she jerked her head from the inspection of the iron flower boxes to study him. Nothing.

That's what greeted her—nothing.

Not a sardonic lift of an eyebrow. Not one of his patented jaded smiles. Not a flicker of emotion as he stood under the mounted glass lamp next to the front door. Just a blank, impenetrable mask. Her stomach twisted with unease. She was missing something here. Something important...

"Over the years, each generation has added to or renovated it. Now it has six bedrooms and bathrooms, four powder rooms, ten fireplaces, an elevator, a rooftop heated pool and garden. There's also a covered patio, three decks, library, media room complete with a home theater, a gym and wine cellar." He rattled off the details and amenities matter-of-factly, impersonally.

"What did you add to it?" she whispered.

He dipped his head, meeting her gaze for the first time since they'd approached the house. "Nothing," he stated, the blunt declaration inviting no questions.

Her heart thudded against her chest, and the same dark sense of dread that had swamped her in the library the night of their engagement party welled up, wrapping its fingers around her throat. Because before Cain turned from her to unlock the front door, she'd caught a bleakness in his eyes. The sight of it stole her breath, sent alarm pounding in her veins.

Something is not right here...

Cain clasped her hand in his and led her into his home and the foyer that could've graced any palace.

Marble floor, crystal chandelier, artwork, beautiful but impractical furniture. It was a showplace that testified to the wealth of its owner. And Cain didn't appear fazed by any of it. His lack of reaction—pride, pleasure, admiration—could be attributed to him growing up here and being immune to it.

But she doubted that was the reason.

An older man in a black suit and white shirt appeared seemingly out of thin air. Even though he didn't stand much taller than her five foot four inches, his military posture lent him the height of a giant.

"I'm sorry I wasn't here to open the door, Mr. Farrell," he apologized, holding his arms out for their coats. "I didn't hear the bell."

"Because I didn't ring it, Ben," Cain replied, his tone and gaze warming. "I have a key, and I'm sure you have more important things to do than running to answer a door I'm fully capable of opening myself." He settled a hand between Devon's shoulder blades, and as if her body recognized the claim her mind rebelled against, she shifted closer to him. "Ben, let me introduce you to my fiancée, Devon Cole. Devon, I'd like you to meet Benjamin Dennis. He's been with my family longer than I have. And he's calling me 'Mr. Farrell' just for your benefit. Usually it's something else less flattering with more colorful language," Cain teased with a snort.

"If you say so, sir," Benjamin drawled, and Devon grinned. "It's a pleasure to meet you, Ms. Cole." He inclined his head, draping their coats over an arm. He swept the other toward the long corridor to the right of the grand staircase. "Your guests are in the great room."

Guests? She frowned. Hadn't Cain said they were having dinner? She'd assumed it would be the two of them.

"Thanks, Ben." Gently applying pressure to her shoulder blades, Cain guided her forward. "This way, Devon."

Still confused, she nonetheless slipped into her polite, social mask—the one she donned when placed in the position of having to talk to people she didn't know. The one she wore while silently counting down the seconds before she could escape.

But the moment she stepped into the entrance of the huge room that could double as a small ballroom, that facade crumbled like dry leaves under a boot.

"Zio Marco. Zia Angela," she breathed, her gaze roaming over the beloved faces of her uncle and aunt. She blinked. But no, they still stood there. More lines around their mouths and eyes, a little more gray hair. But here. Still not believing she was seeing their faces after more than six years, she shifted to the others in the room. "Carla. Beth. Manny." Her cousins. And all of her parents' brothers and sisters and their children. Happiness, shock and a fear that if she glanced away from them, they would disappear swirled inside her. It grew and grew, spinning faster and faster until her chest ached, her throat seized and her eyes stung. "I can't believe... What are you doing here?"

"Devon," her aunt Angela said, dark eyes shining with tears as she moved forward, arms outstretched.

Devon almost ran forward, meeting her halfway. Angela drew Devon close, hugging her. The scent of powder and spices embraced her as well, transporting her back to her childhood. She closed her eyes, pressing her cheek to Angela's shoulder, her arms tightening around the woman who looked so much like her mother both joy and grief pulsed inside her veins.

"We've missed you so much. So much." Leaning back, her mother's sister clasped Devon's face between her soft palms and smiled wide. "When your man called and told us you were engaged, then invited us to see you and meet him, how could we not come?"

Cain... Cradling her aunt's hands, she drew them down and whipped around to face Cain, who remained in the entrance. "You arranged all of this? For me?" she whispered.

"Arranged it?" Zio Marco boomed, appearing beside his wife and throwing an arm around her. "He flew all of us in, put us up in a hotel and provided a limo to bring us here. This one must really love you to shell out money like that just to see you smile, eh?"

God, she'd missed her uncle's lack of filter. She grinned, tears tracking down her cheeks even as a sliver of pain slid between her ribs.

This one must really love you to shell out money like that just to see you smile...

She couldn't begin to grasp why Cain had done this for her but love surely hadn't been the motivation. Right now, though, with her aunts, uncles and cousins noisily gathering around her, she didn't care.

"Have you met Cain yet?" she asked. Twisting at the waist, she stretched her arm toward him, palm up. His gaze settled on hers, and she caught the flicker of emotion that appeared then disappeared before she could decipher it. Still, he strode forward, enclosing her hand in his and stepping to her side. "Everyone, this is Cain Farrell, my fiancé and the person who made all this possible." She squeezed his fingers. "Cain, this is…everyone." She laughed, so much joy inside her, it seemed impossible that her body contained it.

Cain greeted her relatives, and never having met a stranger, they pulled him into the fold without reservation or hesitation—which included hugging him, slapping him on the back, grilling him about his sports allegiances and asking if he had any bachelor friends. This from Zia Stella, who had three daughters. Devon chuckled, enjoying Cain's faintly overwhelmed expression.

No, she didn't understand why he'd gone through all the trouble for tonight.

But he'd given her the best gift.

Family.

Eleven

"I can't thank you enough," Devon said to Cain…
again. For probably the fifteenth time.

And she would say it fifteen more.

Even though her relatives had left five minutes ago,
after a boisterous and prolonged goodbye with promises
to get together tomorrow morning before they left for
New Jersey, Cain's house still seemed to ring with their
voices. "I'll never forget this night. I—" She shook her
head, and once more, murmured, "Thank you."

Cain nodded. "You're welcome, Devon." He studied her for a moment, his blue-gray eyes shuttered yet
intense. "Would you like a drink? Or I can take you
home now."

That invitation shouldn't sound like an offer to sin.
Issued from Cain, it most likely wasn't. But that knowl-

edge didn't prevent a hot pulse of desire from playing slip 'n' slide through her veins. It was late; if she
possessed an iota of intelligence and self-preservation,
she would decline the nightcap and head home. But
enough wine had flowed this evening and she still rode
high on the delight of being with her family. Both were
enough to justify any unwise decisions she made tonight. Besides, it was a drink. She could handle one
drink without committing any acts she would regret
in the morning.

"Do you have any more of the wine from dinner?
The Moscato?" she asked.

"Of course," he said, striding out of the foyer.

She followed him to a smaller, more intimate room
than the one they'd been gathered in for most of the
evening. A couple of couches, a cozy sitting area with
chairs and a low table, a huge fireplace with a stone
mantel, and a built-in bar occupied the space. Choosing
one of the large armchairs in front of the low-burning
flames, she sank down into it as Cain approached her
with a wineglass. He lowered to the matching chair
across from her, and for the next several moments, they
sipped in silence, the muted crackle of wood the only
sound.

"You weren't exaggerating when you said you came
from a big, loud family," Cain said, peering at her over
the rim of his tumbler.

She laughed. "And honestly, I think they went easy
on you because they didn't want to scare you off before
we get married."

As soon as the words exited her mouth, she mentally

winced. *Before we get married* seemed to echo in the room over and over, ratcheting up in volume. God, she hadn't meant to say that. Especially since she still hadn't given up on finding a way out for both of them. How she would accomplish that feat? No clue. She stared down into the depths of her glass as if it held the solution.

"No one mentioned your father. They didn't appear to find it strange that he wasn't there," he added, his scrutiny fixed on her.

Another land mine of a subject. *I don't want to talk about him. Not here and now,* she silently yelled. But Cain had brought up her father, and after all he'd done for her, she couldn't *not* reply.

"I'm not surprised," she admitted softly, shifting her gaze to the fireplace so he couldn't glimpse her shame. "At one time, we were all very close. Even given our family's size, we still managed to be tight. Holidays, birthdays, communions, graduations, hell just because— we spent our days together. The locations might change, but not the people. We were especially close to Uncle Marco and Aunt Angela, my mother's older sister, since they and their family lived on the other side of us in our duplex. But that changed after Mom died. Everything changed," she whispered.

Taking a fortifying drink, she inhaled a deep breath and continued, "I lost Mom, and I lost Dad, too. He used to be such a jokester as well as protective and loving. I couldn't have asked for a better father, a more caring father. But after she died, he became angry, stern and work obsessed. It's like he transferred all the love and grief into building his business. Now I think he worked so hard so he could divorce himself from the life he'd shared with Mom. If he couldn't have her then he would erect an existence that was dramatically different from the one he'd shared with her. He accomplished what he set out to do."

Underneath her joy tonight had lurked a bittersweet sadness. For the memories. For all she'd lost. For the distance she'd allowed to spring between her and her relatives out of a misplaced loyalty to her father. He'd essentially forced her to choose; she'd chosen her remaining living parent.

"The more successful Dad's business became, the more he distanced himself from our family. First, it was moving out of the duplex. Then out of Plainfield. Then out of New Jersey. He cut them out of his life as efficiently and effectively as slicing off a limb. They no longer fit who Gregory Cole had shaped himself into, didn't fit into the world he'd created."

"What about you? He decided to purge his life of them, why did you have to?" Cain demanded, leaning forward and propping his elbows on his thighs, cupping the squat glass in his strong hands. She focused on those hands so she wouldn't catch the condemnation in his eyes.

"I didn't have to," she said, guilt and embarrassment thickening her voice. "Dad only had me. Mom died and he no longer had his brothers, sisters or in-laws, even though, yes, that was by his own decision. It was just us. And…" She swallowed hard, battling the conditioned response to defend her father even when he was indefensible. Inhaling a shuddering breath, she shoved the truth past her suddenly constricted throat. "And I promised my mother on her deathbed that I would look after my dad. And that included not abandoning him even though he'd abandoned his family."

Abandoned me.

"I didn't know your mother, but from how your aunts and uncles spoke about her at dinner, I feel like I'm more familiar with her than I was before tonight. A woman who loved to cook huge meals, so she feeds everyone... A woman whose heart and joy were her child and husband and providing a haven for them... A woman who has been gone for over fifteen years, but who her family still remembers with love and reverence... That woman wouldn't have wanted her daughter to not know the safety and happiness of family. And she didn't intend for you to carry the burden of your father's decisions or make them your own. No child—whether two or eighty-two—should be placed in that ugly and unfair position."

She stared at him, trembling. An automatic objection to his assurance swelled in her but desperation silenced it. Desperation to grab on to those words and absorb them as truth. Desperation to be freed by them.

Closing her eyes, she willed the stinging to recede. Her fingers tightened around the wineglass, and afraid of shattering it in her grip, she set it on the low table between their chairs.

"Devon, look at me." The low, tender command contained a thread of steel, and she obeyed it. "When I called your aunt, do you know what she said after I told her who I was?" She shook her head, unable to voice anything. In the firelight, his bright gaze softened. "She said she'd been waiting for this phone call. She hadn't known who it would come from or when it would happen, but that she never doubted she would one day have you back. Not once did she give up on you, and there was no bitterness, no resentment. Just pure happiness that she would see you again. Sweetheart," he murmured, "they don't blame you. So stop beating yourself up."

"Why did you do this?" she blurted out. One, because the question had been nagging her all evening. And two, she needed a distraction before she asked him to hold her.

He was the last person she should be asking for comfort.

But in this moment, he was the only one she wanted.

How pathetic did that make her?

"At the community center, you gave me a few moments of happiness. Maybe I wanted to do the same for you. Or..." He glanced at the fireplace, and in its light, she noted the jump of a muscle along the clenched line of his jaw. "This house has never been a...happy one. Maybe I was just being selfish and wanted to steal some of what you have with your family. Even if for a little while."

Images of his cold expression, of the desolation in his eyes as they approached his home earlier flashed in her mind. What had happened here?

Longer than I can remember. That had been his response when she'd asked him how long it'd been since he'd truly enjoyed himself. For someone who possessed wealth, power and a blue blood pedigree, he seemed so isolated…so lonely.

It was wrong. This man who had sent dozens of pizzas to a center full of kids, granting them great memories, should be offered the same selflessness in return. This man who would surrender his own happiness and future to protect his mother from humiliation should be given the same protection. This man who'd reunited her with her family just to bring her joy was deserving of that same joy.

Even if for a little while, as he'd said.

Her pulse pounded under her skin, the blood in her veins suddenly screaming, hot and *alive*. She could do that for him.

Staring at him, at the slight frown that indented his brows, at the thick fringe of lashes that hid the emotion in his beautiful eyes…at the bold, carnal slant of his firm mouth…

She *needed* to do that for him.

Her breath whistled through her lungs, but she still slid to the edge of her chair. Then lower, to her knees.

As if Cain caught her movement out of his peripheral vision, his head jerked around, his wolf's gaze narrowing on her. Surprise glinted in the bright depths. Surprise and hunger. Oh God, so much hunger. Its heat warmed her skin more than the flames from the fireplace, and for a moment, she hesitated.

Would that intensity consume her? Leave her as ash? *Yes.*

The answer was immediate and unequivocal.

And it would be her fault. She knew the consequences of playing with fire. She could turn back now before she crawled too far onto this path. She could end this, return to her seat and blame this impulsive decision on the wine...

She shifted forward on her knees—in supplication.

He didn't move except for the flare of his nostrils. Did he scent the desire that threatened to incinerate her? Silly question, but here, with lust an invisible string between them, yanking her closer, she could afford a bit of whimsy. It kept her from focusing on the reality of what she courted—a sexual animal who could easily devour her.

The short, negligible distance between her chair and his seemed to stretch for miles, but she finally reached him. Settling her hands on his knees, she applied pressure, widening his thighs. He allowed it, his muscles bunching then relaxing as he slowly opened for her, straightening when she claimed more space for herself. Only when his legs bracketed either side of her torso did she stop.

And she slid her arms around his waist, pressing her cheek to the wide, solid expanse of his chest.

Cain stiffened, but she didn't loosen her embrace, didn't pull back. Desire continued to throb inside her but even more than she craved his mouth on her, she craved holding him. She needed to offer him the comfort he'd so selflessly given her. And whether he admitted it or not, he needed to be held.

In slow increments, his arms rose. Wrapped around her. Tightened. Gripped.

His big body curled over hers, sheltering her even

as he clung to her. With her height—or lack of it—his
frame nearly doubled over to hold her close. The position couldn't have been comfortable, but he didn't let
go. No, he buried his face in the crook of her neck, his
heavy puffs of air bathing her skin. Each beat of her
pulse transmitted an insatiable greed through her, but
she closed her eyes, focusing on the power of the body
surrounding her. On the fresh, earth-and-wood scent
filling her nose. She inhaled, already taking him inside her.

An inarticulate groan rumbled up and out of him,
and she felt the vibration before the sound reached her
ears. He jerked out of her embrace with an almost painful wrench and glared down at her, face taut over his
sharp cheekbones, his mouth a hard, cruel line.

"What do you want from me?" he snapped, chest
rising and falling as if he'd just barreled across a great
distance.

"What are you willing to give?" she asked, not in-
timidated by the abrupt switch in his emotions. Not
hindered by the soft voice in her head that warned she
was turning into one of those people willing to settle
for scraps. She shushed that voice. Afraid if she didn't,
she would realize it was right.

"Nothing," he growled, his fingers tunneling under
the loose knot at the back of her head, tugging on the
strands and freeing them. "Everything," he hissed, tone
rougher...angrier.

With her or himself? She couldn't tell. And in that
second, with his blunt fingertips dragging down her

scalp and pleasure sucking her into its depths, she didn't care. Just as long as he didn't let her surface.

"And what are you willing to give me, Devon?" he challenged, trailing a caress from the dip in her collarbone, up the front of her throat, over her chin and to her lips. Leaving fire in its wake. His other hand, twisted in her hair, drew her head back farther, arching her neck tighter as he traced the outline of her mouth. As his finger breached her, sliding over her tongue and then withdrawing to paint her trembling flesh with her own moisture.

"What I can afford to," she whispered, the answer containing a raw honesty she hadn't meant to reveal.

But from the heat blazing in his eyes like a strike of lightning, he coveted it.

"I'll take it," he said then crushed his mouth to hers.

On a ragged moan, she opened for him, welcomed the demanding thrust of his tongue. Eagerly, she returned the hard, rough sucking. He came at her like a starving man and she was his only sustenance. Not gentle, no manners. Just ravenous and desperate. Wild.

She tore away, gulping in a breath, but he didn't allow it. He followed her, his lips covering hers again, almost bruising in their greed. The hand not gripping her hair lowered to her neck, circling the front and mimicking the caress from the library. And just like then, lust flared hotter, brighter. Her nipples beaded under her dress, and she cupped her breasts, squeezed, attempting to alleviate the ache.

"Dammit, that's pretty," Cain praised, lifting his head and staring down at her kneading hands. He palmed her arms and guided her to her feet. Instinctively, Devon grasped for his shoulders, but he cuffed her wrists and returned her hands to her chest. "Don't stop," he ordered, waiting until she resumed her self-ministrations before freeing his grip.

His searing gaze only ratcheted up the clawing need raging through her, not easing it. Whimpering, she rubbed her thumbs over the distended tips, barely aware of him removing her shoes and tugging down her zipper. Air kissed the skin of her back, and she gasped. He drew the sleeves down her arms, her bra swiftly following, and seconds later, she stood half-naked in front of him.

It occurred to her that she should feel some embarrassment being so bared and vulnerable. Especially when her figure resembled nothing close to those of the women she'd seen him with. But, as he stared down at her breasts, the pure lust in those blue-gray eyes banished any doubts or insecurities that would've crept in.

He wanted her.

No matter what had brought them together. No matter how much he might resent this and her later… He wanted her.

And for now, it was enough. Had to be.

For both of them.

"So beautiful," he murmured, stroking up her waist and pausing just under her breasts. Leaning forward, he brushed his lips over her jaw, sweeping another caress just under her ear. "Tell me to touch you, sweetheart. Tell me to give us both what we need."

"Touch me," she whispered. No hesitation. No reservation. "Give us both what we need. And don't hold back."

If tonight was going to be all they had before returning to opposing sides, then she wanted no regrets.

She wanted the everything he'd promised her.

A growl rolled out of him, and his hands rose, claiming her breasts. "I was right." He squeezed her flesh, plumping it, molding it to his palms. Biting her bottom lip to hold back the tiny scream scaling her throat, she settled for sinking her nails into his forearms. And holding on. His gaze lifted from her nipples to her mouth, and then higher to meet her eyes. "You more than fill my hands. I can't number how many times I've woken up, my fist around my dick, picturing it. Wondering if my imagination neared reality. It didn't. Reality is so much better."

Before the shock that he dreamed about her could ebb, his mouth was on her. Tugging, sucking deep, swirling, giving her the barest graze of his teeth. She clutched him—clawed at him—her head thrown back as every swipe of his tongue, every pull on the beaded, overly sensitive tip, echoed in her sex.

This had always been pleasurable in the past, but *God…* He shoved her toward the precarious edge of orgasm, and until this moment, she hadn't known it was possible to come from a man's mouth on her breasts.

No, not a man.

Cain.

His ravenous mouth shifted, and cool air teased her wet flesh as he engulfed the other aching peak. Whimper after whimper escaped her, and she arched higher, harder into him, granting him access to all of her. Wordlessly begging him to take more, give her more.

And he did.

Just as she demanded, he didn't hold back, and the first tight contraction in her sex took her by surprise. She gasped, then cried out, her thighs tightening, hips jerking as pleasure swelled and cracked.

Harsh puffs of air wheezed out of her lungs, and she shook not just with the orgasm that gripped her, but with shock. That had never happened to her. And before she could tamp it down, a thread of despair wormed its way into her head. Sex wouldn't be the same after this. Already he'd redefined the experience, exposing her to things about herself, her body that she hadn't understood. Now Cain would be the yardstick by which she measured every person after him.

And she suspected—feared—no one would measure up.

His rough chuckle tickled her skin as he lifted his head, lips slightly reddened and damp. Lust blazed in his bright eyes. Lust and a glowing satisfaction. "You need another one, don't you, sweetheart?" he damn near purred, his thumbs still whisking back and forth over her nipples, making her shift and twist underneath his tormenting hands. "That just took the edge off."

Helplessly, she nodded. Because, dammit, she still *hurt*.

He pressed a hard, but thoroughly erotic kiss to her mouth, his tongue diving deep and rubbing against hers, obliterating all thought except for the hunger he ignited within her. Each parry and thrust was an explicit promise of what he still had in store for her. She opened wider for him and slid her hands through his hair. Gripping them, she guided his head, tilting it, so she could do her fair share of conquering. His dark groan telegraphed his approval.

One moment, she stood there, devouring his mouth, and in the next, the world upended as Cain wrapped his arms around her, hauled her off her feet and bore her to the thickly carpeted floor. By the time she regained her breath, he'd tugged the dress gathered at her waist down her legs. Black lace panties quickly followed. Only the flames and his searing hot gaze licked over her skin, heating her.

She shivered, and a belated bout of modesty materialized. One hand fluttered restlessly over her chest—which made zero sense considering he'd just had his lips and tongue there—and the other settled on her rounded belly, inching toward the soaked, swollen flesh between her thighs. She was so exposed. So naked. So vulnerable. Emphasized even more by the suit he still wore. He'd shed her of her armor, put every imperfection and insecurity of hers on display. But he remained as guarded, as *safe* as ever.

She didn't like it.

"Take it off," she croaked.

She hadn't planned on issuing that order, and from the stillness of his big frame, he hadn't expected it either. Maybe he didn't appreciate it, if the narrowing of his eyes provided any indication. But she didn't rescind the demand. They needed to be on equal footing tonight. It was all she would accept.

"The suit," she clarified. "Take it off."

He didn't move, and for an instant, panic bubbled within her chest. Had she gone too far? Would he walk away? A man so used to power and being in charge probably didn't take kindly to another person attempting to wrestle control from him. Well, it would hurt, but if he chose to leave, then he did. Tonight was about what they both needed, not just what he needed.

But her worries dissipated as he wrenched his tie from side to side, loosening the knot. The material fluttered to the floor. And his jacket, shirt, socks and shoes followed. At the sight of his wide, powerful chest and shoulders, and his ruthlessly toned arms, she swallowed past a constricted throat. Constricted with the rawest, most primitive need that had ever gripped her.

He was…perfect.

From the jut of his collarbone, to the dusting of dark hair over his pectorals, to the intriguing, dusky dip of his navel, on to the silky line bisecting his corrugated abs that disappeared under the band of his pants.

Sculpted art. Battle-ready warrior.

And for tonight, *mine*.

Oh, she should be terrified at how that one word resonated inside her. Instead, her fingertips itched to trace every beautiful inch of him.

But his hooded stare pinned her in place as his hands fell to the top of his pants. Without removing his gaze from her, he unbuttoned and unzipped his pants, then shoved them down his muscular thighs. She had just enough time to soak in his beauty clothed only in tight black boxer briefs when he pushed those down, too.

And *oh my God…*

Had she thought him stunning before? She'd been mistaken.

Stripped of the layers of civility, the true primal, beautiful animal was revealed. If anything, the cloak of his suits muted the power so evident in his big, naked body. She stared. Couldn't help it. Even that part of him—almost brutish with its wide, flared cap and thick, veined column—was gorgeous. And her mouth watered for a taste. To see if the virility that emanated from him possessed a particular flavor…

She didn't realize she'd shifted to her elbows, prepared to discover the truth for herself, until he knelt between her legs and pressed a palm to her shoulder, gently lowering her back down. A graze of lips over her neck, a kiss to each nipple, a nip of her stomach, a lick of her hip bone… Alarm scaled in her chest as understanding struck her. Belatedly, she scrabbled for his shoulders, but he moved out of her reach.

In her experience, oral sex seemed a chore for men. And in return, it'd never been that much of a pleasurable act because their impatience hindered her from truly enjoying it. The thought of disappointing Cain with her lack of reaction sent a trill of panic through her. Why couldn't they just get to the main event? Him inside her—

Oh…

Cain dragged a long, luxurious lick up the center of her, circling the pulsing nub cresting the top of her sex. Pleasure bolted through her and her hips punched upward, meeting his tongue and lips. A groan ripped free from her, and a full-body shudder worked its way over her.

"God, you taste good," Cain muttered, delivering another hot suck. Another flick. "The only thing I wanted more than this was to be buried so fucking deep inside you. And breathing. Maybe. If I could have this every day—" another soft and brutal lick "—breathing might be optional."

His words whirled in her head, echoed in her chest even as Cain's mouth yanked her under his erotic spell. She tunneled her fingers in his hair, gripping the strands as he feasted on her. His hum vibrated against her flesh, and it hit her that he was *enjoying it*. Enjoying *her*.

He claimed every inch of her with his greedy strokes, licks and swirls. She lost herself in the dark pool of ecstasy, willingly going under with each nibble and lap.

"Cain," she rasped. Hell, pleaded.

In reply, he drew her into his mouth, sucked hard and thrust a finger inside her.

She flew.

She seized, the rapture tearing at her, splintering her. The piercing sound of her cry reverberated in the room, and she couldn't be embarrassed about it. Not when pleasure unlike any she'd known arced through her in jagged waves. She could barely breathe past it, her frame trembling as it ebbed.

Lethargy soaked into her muscles, but then the sight of Cain snatching his jacket close, retrieving his billfold from the inside pocket and removing a small foil packet ignited the simmering heat in her veins, in her flesh.

He stared down at her, bright eyes an almost unholy

glow, skin pulled taut over his cheekbones, his glistening mouth hard. With deft movements, he sheathed himself and she lifted her arms, reaching for him. Inviting him. Welcoming him.

His hands flattened on either side of her hips, and he crawled over her, not stopping until his mouth hovered above hers. And when he crashed his lips to hers, his tongue sliding over hers, dueling, making her taste herself on him, she didn't resist. No, she took, took, took.

"Ask me to come in," he growled against her.

She circled her arms around his neck and rolled her desperate, throbbing sex over him. "Please," she whimpered, nipping his chin, his bottom lip and kissing the sting from both of them. "Come inside me. Make the emptiness go away."

No sooner did the plea escape her, than he plunged. Stretching her. Filling her.

Branding her.

Nothing could've prepared her for him. For the strength of him. The power of him. Of this sense of completion.

"Breathe, sweetheart," he grated in her ear. And on a gust, she released the breath she hadn't known she'd been holding, her pulse thumping in her ears. "You okay?" He brushed a kiss over her brow, the bridge of her nose and finally, her mouth. "I won't move until you tell me to."

She shifted beneath him, and *oh God*. "Move," she gasped. Winding her legs around his waist, she undulated beneath him, and another cry broke free. "Move now."

He didn't ask her if she was sure, just took her at her word. Like the reins tethering his control had snapped, he withdrew from her until only the tip stretched her opening. Then buried himself inside her, propelling a scream from her lungs.

"So good," she breathed. "Too good."

"Never," he grunted, his hips grinding against hers, directly over the bundle of nerves where pleasure coiled and pulsed. "It's never too good."

Curling a hand behind her neck, he crushed his mouth to hers, taking her lips even as his steel-hard flesh took her body. He drove into her, riding her, molding her to him so that she fit only him. Craved only him. As she arched beneath him, writhing and bucking, she knew, *knew*, that he'd ruined her for anyone else. No one had ever made her feel as if she were dying and being reborn at the same time.

She dug her fingernails into his taut shoulders, moaning into his mouth. He swallowed the sound and gave her back his own in return. There wasn't any way she could survive this. Not intact. But as he powered into her, hooking a hand under her knee and pushing her leg toward her chest so he could bury himself deeper, she couldn't care.

"Cain." She jerked her head back, pressed it against the floor. "Please."

"Look at me," he growled, pinching her chin and tugging her back down to meet his lust-brightened eyes. "Look at me and let go."

With his dark command and a grind of the base of his cock over her sex, she did. She let go and shattered. Just fragmented into so many pieces it should've scared her. But she felt only the purity of pleasure…and freedom.

She fell into the abyss, and as Cain stiffened and thrust in broken, desperate strokes, she knew neither one of them would be alone.

At least not for tonight.

Twelve

Cain studied the road before him, the white dotted lines blurring under his focus. At one o'clock in the morning, Boston might not have been asleep but little traffic cluttered the streets from Beacon Hill to Back Bay. The drive should take only ten minutes. But with the woman sitting silently beside him in the car and the tension thick, the trip stretched for much longer.

He couldn't decide if he longed for this drive to be over, or to prolong it until he could empty himself of the confusion, remorse, guilt—and *need*—stretching him so thin one move might snap him in two.

Goddammit, he should've never touched her.

Never put his mouth on her.

Never slid deep into a body so soft and tight he'd

been both embraced and strangled. Been caressed and bruised. Been drained dry and strengthened.

Devon had fucked not only his body but his mind. She'd left him trembling like a damn colt on unfamiliar legs. And yet, as he'd eased out of her, regretting the loss of her snug, quivering sex, he'd been…alive. For the first time in, God, so many years. Blood had sung through his veins as if he'd just returned from battle. He'd been euphoric and yes, at peace.

He'd had sex before. And it'd been pleasurable, fun, even dirty at times. But never had it humbled him. Invigorated him. Twisted him in so many knots he resembled a snarled ball of yarn.

Never had it begun with a hug that nearly broke him so every secret, every fear and longing poured out of the cracks.

But then, he'd never had sex with Devon Cole before.

It couldn't happen again.

Touching the curves that had been driving him crazy from their first meeting and mapping their sweetness with his hands and mouth had been a beautiful mistake. But it'd been a mistake nonetheless.

He'd lowered his guard, made himself vulnerable in a way that was just short of unforgivable. With any other woman, sex would've been a natural, biological release. But Devon was far from "any other woman." She was the daughter of the man who blackmailed him and threatened his mother. She was the daughter complicit in her father's machinations, and even though she hadn't issued the ultimatum, she benefited from Gregory's deceit and schemes.

Cain couldn't forgive or forget that. Only a fool would turn a blind eye to the wolf snarling and snapping at his door. And though he'd been played for one by Devon in his mother's garden, he wouldn't make that error again. Barron had committed a multitude of sins—abused his son, cheated on his wife, abandoned and hid away children—but he hadn't raised a fool.

"I know you're already regretting having sex with me," Devon said, her low, husky voice like a cannon blast in the silence of the car.

He yanked his attention from the road and glanced at her. But Devon stared out the passenger-side window, giving him a view of the long, thick hair tumbling over her shoulders and back.

"I just have one question for you," she said.

"What is it?" he asked, not denying her assertion that he regretted being with her.

Material rustled, and when he shifted another look in her direction, she'd turned to face him. Shadows danced over her face, casting her in both darkness and the light from the streetlamps. But her careful, composed expression betrayed none of her thoughts.

Resentment ignited inside his chest before he deliberately snuffed it out. A part of him wanted her to appear as agitated and unsettled as he felt.

"You once listed the things I wouldn't receive from you in this…arrangement. Fidelity was one of them. You would have sex with other women, but not with me." She inhaled, and Cain fought the urge to wrap a hand around the nape of her neck, draw her close. He tightened his grip on the steering wheel, the other hand on his thigh curling into a fist. "Tonight," she continued, "was that about you using me to further stick it to my father? Do I need to prepare myself to have this thrown in his face—and mine—at some point? Because if so, I—"

"Let's get one thing straight, sweetheart," he growled, cutting her off. "Your father uses women as pawns in his little games—I don't. You were underneath me on that floor, Devon. You came for me. *You.* The only agenda I had tonight was getting as far deep inside you as I could, and that had *nothing* to do with your father."

A heartbeat of quiet passed, thunderous and heavy. And so dense with desire it pressed against his skin. His cock twitched against his thigh.

Damn, this was his fault.

He shouldn't have mentioned her coming for him, because now he swore he could feel the phantom spasms of her slick flesh around him. The craving to have it again, to have her surrounding him, burned him.

Hungering for his enemy's daughter only spelled trouble. So no matter how hard his dick throbbed and complained, tonight had been the first and last time.

"I believe you," she murmured.

He shot her a glare. "Then you're a fool," he snapped. Ignoring her sharp intake of breath, he pressed her. "You and I aren't friends. We aren't lovers. Tonight might not have been about your father but that doesn't mean I won't destroy him and fuck the casualties. Even if one of those casualties is you. Don't believe me.

Don't trust me. Because I damn sure don't trust you or Gregory."

He thrust his free hand through his hair, grinding his teeth together. *Lie.* The word whistled through his head. His father had been that ruthless. That coldhearted, to allow an innocent to be harmed in the course of business.

All his life, Cain's one goal hadn't been to run Farrell International as its CEO. It had been to be nothing like Barron Farrell.

But she isn't innocent.

Images of her in the garden, at the community center, of her crawling across that floor to hug him flickered across his mind like camera flashes. That Devon contradicted the woman he'd seen in her father's living room, who'd stood silently as Cain challenged her to repudiate Gregory's plans. To free them both. And she hadn't. No, the last few hours proved that she desired him, but she obviously desired the Farrell name and connections more.

Once, that knowledge had enraged him, hauling out the emotional baggage of his childhood.

Now, though? Now he was just…*tired.*

"I'm not naive, Cain," she said, turning back to the window. He hated the even tone that betrayed none of the hurt he'd heard in that little gasp. "I trusted you with my body tonight, but nothing else. I'm not a fool now, but I was once upon a time. And thank you for the reminder of what could happen if I forget that."

What the hell are you talking about? Who were you

*a fool for? What happened to put that hollow note in
your voice?*

The barrage of questions slammed a path toward
his throat, clamoring to emerge and desperate for her
answers. But he locked them down. He didn't have the
right to ask. But that didn't prevent a dark, ugly emotion with claws from tearing at him.

Jealousy.

He didn't even bother with the pretense of denying
its existence. The snarling, green-eyed beast in him
wanted, *demanded* she confess this other man's name,
the details of what he'd done...if she'd loved him.

Dammit.

He scrubbed a hand down his face, his five-o'clock
shadow abrading his palm. He had no claims on her,
regardless of the contract his father and Gregory had
signed.

He needed distance, space to get himself back in
check. Under control. Yes, control was key. Not losing
his temper with his father or betraying any of his hurt
had become an art form for Cain. After years of practice,
not losing it over a woman he'd known for a handful of
weeks was child's play.

"Good," he said, guiding his car down her quiet,
dark street. "We're in agreement, then. Tonight was a
mistake. One we can't repeat."

His life contained enough complications with brothers he barely knew, a company to run and an inheri-
tance to lock down.

And a mausoleum of a house to return to with only
screaming childhood ghosts for company.

No, he didn't need anything else on his plate. Like an inappropriate and inconvenient fascination for a woman with eyes like emeralds, a Mona Lisa face and the curves of a goddess.

"Of course," Devon said. "Business as usual. We both know how good I am at following orders."

The comment referred to how she so easily conformed to her father's dictates, but that's not how his body interpreted it.

Don't stop.

Breathe, sweetheart.

Look at me and let go.

She'd followed those orders so sweetly, too.

Lust rippled through him when he remembered how he'd obeyed hers as well.

Take it off.

Her husky, sensual words echoed in his ears, and he steeled himself against the wave of need that crashed over him. Silently uttering a curse, he jerked the gearshift into Park and damn near bolted out of the car.

Distance and space. Distance and space.

The two words became his mantra as he rounded the car to open her door. But she'd already pushed it open and stepped out, heading for the front steps of the townhome.

"You don't need to walk me to the door," she objected in that cool voice that set his teeth on edge. Even though it was what he needed to keep her in the neat box where he'd placed her.

"I'm walking you to the door, Devon," he ground out,

his hand hovering over the small of her back. But after a moment, he lowered it. Better off not tempting fate by touching her at all. Not with their mingled scents still clinging to his skin. "You're not some booty call that's dropped off at the curb."

"I'm not a friend. I'm not a lover. And now I'm not a booty call," she said, fishing her key out of her purse and sliding it into the slot. "I'm beginning to wonder who or what I am." She grabbed the knob and twisted. Even as his mind ordered him to avoid putting his hands on her, he cupped her elbow, halting her.

She didn't turn around, and he didn't force her to. Instead, he edged closer until his chest pressed to her back and his reawakened cock nudged the rise of her ass. He clenched his jaw against the pleasure and pain of the contact. Against the insatiable animal inside him that roared for more.

He lowered his head. "You're a beautiful, unwanted, sexy-as-fuck complication," he growled.

Then he stepped back. Away from temptation. Away from whatever pull she had on his will and his body.

Away from her.

Without looking back, he strode down the steps and the front walk to his car. Once he was inside the safe confines of the vehicle, he glanced at Devon, standing in the doorway. Due to the distance and the shadows, he couldn't decipher every feature of her face, couldn't see her eyes. There was no possible way she could note his regard through the heavily tinted windows, but only when he stared at her, did she walk through the entrance and close the door behind her.

Shutting herself in.

Shutting him out.

Thirteen

Being up at eight o'clock on a Sunday morning should have been considered a punishable offense, but having breakfast with her family before they returned to New Jersey pardoned her crime.

She smiled, excitement and happiness spilling over as she pulled on her jacket and descended the stairs to the foyer. Already, she'd talked to her aunt Angela, and the other woman's steady flow of chatter and laughter had been infectious. Devon had needed to finally tell her aunt that she had to hang up and get dressed or she would be late meeting them at their hotel.

Devon shook her head, her smile faltering. When Zia Angela had informed her of the exact hotel where they were staying, she'd swallowed a surprised gasp. The five-star hotel catered to the wealthiest and most famous, and Cain had arranged for her huge family to stay there like they were royalty. Regardless of how their evening had ended last night after having sex, she was so grateful to him for his treatment of her family.

And no, she preferred not to dwell on that awkward, cold ride home. As soon as the sweat dried on their skin, he'd seemed eager to be rid of her. And his insistence that what had been special to her was nothing but a momentary lapse in judgment—that she was a *beautiful, unwanted, sexy-as-fuck complication*—had scored her deeper than it should have. Deeper than she wanted to admit.

It'd required every bit of acting ability she possessed not to loose her anger, or worse, her tears.

She'd *known*.

God, she'd known that he could inflict damage on her. But she'd convinced herself that she wouldn't lower her guard.

All the good that'd done her.

Pausing on the bottom step, she briefly closed her eyes. She wanted to rail against Cain, to accuse him of using her. But…she couldn't. This—the hollow, gut-punched feeling weighing her down—could, and should, be laid entirely at her feet.

Donald had taught her to believe her eyes, her logic, not her heart. For hours last night, she'd stared up at her ceiling, unable to sleep, silently reprimanding herself for forgetting.

She wouldn't forget again.

"Devon, good. You're awake." Her father drew to a stop at the base of the staircase, his gaze skimming over her short leather jacket, white T-shirt, jeans and ankle boots. "Where are you going so early?"

The "looking like that" remained unsaid but was heard loud and clear.

She considered lying. Confrontation did not top her list of favorite things, especially with her father. But she'd given in to her father once where her family was concerned and lost them for years. Not again.

"I'm headed downtown to meet up with Zia Angela, Zio Marco and the rest of the family for breakfast."

Shock blanked his handsome features. But then anger poured in, mottling his cheeks and thinning his mouth. "Excuse me?"

"I said that I'm—"

"I heard you," he snapped, slicing a hand through the air. "But I don't want to believe it's true. What are *they* doing here in Boston?"

She detested the derision in his voice when referring to his brothers and sisters—his wife's family—as if they were beneath him. All because they were poor, and he now had money and a home in a certain zip code.

"They're here because Cain invited them here, and because I wanted to see them. We all had dinner together last night, and it would've been wonderful if you'd been there, too. They miss you."

"Is that why you two didn't show up at the opening last night? Because you were entertaining them?" His lips twisted into an ugly sneer. "Cain had no business interfering in our family affairs. Your aunts and uncles don't belong here, not in our world. And I thought you understood that, Devon."

"*Our family*, Dad?" Devon shook her head, loosing a short, incredulous laugh. "I understand that I distanced myself from them to please you, even if it hurt me. Even if I missed them with every breath. Besides you, they are my last connection to Mom. They're yours, too, but maybe that's why you cut them out of our lives. Because you don't want to be reminded of Mom. And because you resent them for reminding you of where we came from. Of why all these blue-blooded assholes won't accept us into their inner circle." She stepped down, meeting her father's glare even though that same fear of disappointing him pumped through her veins. "Well, you can continue to deny their existence, but I'm not going to throw away this chance of getting to know them again. And if that upsets you, well…"

She shrugged and started past her father, but he grasped her elbow. "We're not finished with this conversation. But I have more important matters to discuss with you. Come to my study."

He released her and, pivoting sharply on his heel, stalked down the hall.

I don't have time for this.

Pulling her cell phone from her back pocket, she peered down at the screen. If she left in ten minutes, she would just make it to the hotel on time. She glanced at the front door, then huffing out a breath, turned and followed her father. Nine minutes. That's all she would give him.

"Close the door behind you," he ordered as she stepped into the study.

She did as he requested and crossed the room to his

desk. "Could we make this quick, Dad? I don't want to be late."

"It will take as long as it takes," he snapped, his fingers drumming impatiently on the desktop. "This takes precedence over your breakfast." He paused, studying her. "Where are you with convincing Cain to invite me to be an investor on his real estate project?"

She stared at him, disbelief and frustration seething inside her. "Really? Are you serious?" she demanded. "I told you I wouldn't bring that up to him, and I didn't. Cain wants nothing to do with you, and there's nothing I could say to convince him otherwise even if I wanted to. Which I don't."

"We discussed this," he persisted, waving off her response as if it were an annoying pest. "You have more influence than you believe. Where's your confidence? And Cain bringing his future father-in-law into his business deals would only bolster the appearance of solidarity and a happy union. *Think*, Devon. Stop being so passive."

Five…four…three… She inhaled a deep breath and forcibly shoved her temper down. Losing it never worked when dealing with her father.

"Cain doesn't care about appearances. He doesn't want—"

"I don't give a damn what he wants," he barked, jabbing a finger into the desk. "I need this, Devon. It's not like he doesn't have other projects. This is any other deal for him, while it means everything to me. To us. To my business."

"Dad," she whispered, dread and foreboding squirming in her stomach. "What are you talking about? What's going on?"

He looked away from her, jaw clenched tight. Several seconds later, he returned his narrowed regard to her, and the anger and— *Oh God*—flicker of fear in his green eyes deepened her unease. "I've made several… unwise investments over the last couple of years, and they've had devastating effects on the firm. Our financial situation is dire. I need a new, reliable project guaranteed to bring in profit for my clients and the company. If I don't…"

Ruin. Bankruptcy. Scandal.

Panic and worry for her father churned inside her. "Oh Dad. I'm so sorry. I had no idea…"

"Now you do," he said, voice clipped. Then he sighed, and for a moment, he looked so tired, so beaten down, that she took a step toward him, needing to hug him, offer some comfort. But his face hardened, and he hiked up his chin, his stare pinning her in place. "You understand now why I need you to persuade him to let me in on this deal. And if you can't convince him, then find some way to obtain the bidding information so I can submit a proposal with a winning bid."

Disgust and horror expelled any sympathy for her father. "You can't mean that, Dad," she rasped. "You can't possibly mean that."

"Devon, you will do this. I'm your father and your first priority. Your loyalty doesn't belong to a man you've known for weeks, and who would toss you aside in a hot second if not for me forcing him to stay with you. Everything you have right now is because of me.

Including that man. Like I told you before, you owe me. Your allegiance. Your duty. Your *life*. All of it, you owe to me."

"And what if the cost is too high?" she demanded, his words splinters that burrowed deep. She didn't need to be reminded of Cain's disdain, his desire to be free of her. Last night had demonstrated that quite clearly. "This isn't about loyalty. This is about your need for more, more, more. More wealth. More status. More connections. More recognition. You've already sunk so low as to use a man's mother to blackmail him into bending to your will. Now you want me to deceive him, spy on him, *steal* from him. What about my integrity? My soul? Because they would be the price I paid if I went through with your plan. And let's be clear. I'm. Not."

"Stop being so dramatic," he sneered and yanked open a drawer, withdrawing a sheet of paper and sliding it across the desk toward her. "Pick it up, read it."

Hesitant, she complied. A list of about twenty names partially covered the sheet. She recognized a few of them as prominent businessmen, but that was it.

"What is this?" she asked, lifting her attention from the paper and meeting her father's gaze.

A smugness curved his lips. That expression could mean nothing good for her.

"That is only a partial list of the donors for your community center, but they are the ones who have donated the most money. It will only take one call from me and a word about how their funds are being mismanaged. All it will require is one person to start withdrawing their money before the others fall like dominoes. And

Devon, that person will be me. The center won't continue without the financial support of its benefactors." He nodded toward the paper she now clutched in her hands like a lifeline.

The names on that list comprised the life support for the place she loved. The place that was the heartbeat of its neighborhood.

"It's your choice," her father continued, arrogance and a sickening self-satisfaction reeking from him like a pungent cologne. "Either do this small favor for me and save your family's company and future. Or stand by and watch me dismantle the center dollar by dollar."

She'd asked herself before who her father had become? Now she had the answer.

He was no longer her mother's husband.

He was a cruel stranger who had passed down his DNA.

Without another word to him, she pivoted and exited the study. Escaped him.

But there was no avoiding the sordid choice he'd left her with.

Either she destroyed lives by eliminating employment, classes, services and a haven for children and seniors.

Or she betrayed a man who despised her family and didn't trust her in the first place.

A breath shuddered out of her, and a vise constricted her chest, her ribs and lungs.

By the time this was over, Cain would hate her even more.

Fourteen

"We have the updated plans and numbers on the North Station project. I've emailed them to you. For those dinosaurs who insist on paper copies, I have those, too."

Laughter filled the room as Karina Douglas, Farrell International's chief financial officer, stood at the head of the conference room table and waved toward the pile of manila folders. "I've also forwarded the latest proposals and bids and a projection for the next three years required to finish the construction and leasing."

Cain tapped his inbox on his tablet and located the email. He opened the attachment and in seconds, numbers filled the screen. This project would mean a very healthy profit for not just Farrell but its investors and stockholders. But the information might as well have been written in hieroglyphics. Nothing made sense or snagged his attention for very long.

Not exactly the truth.

There was one person who monopolized his thoughts and attention. Had thoroughly hijacked his focus so not even work offered an escape. Which was unprecedented. No person or thing had ever interfered with work before. He hadn't allowed it. But since Saturday night—since he'd dropped Devon off at her house with both of them still smelling of sex—he didn't have a choice.

Devon Cole had become his own personal ghost. And she haunted him when he was awake and during the few hours of sleep he managed to snatch.

His fingers tightened around the stylus, and it pressed into his skin. Nearly forty-eight hours had passed since he'd last seen her, and he could still hear her moans in his ears. Still feel the impatient, demanding twist of her body under his. Still smell the perfume of her need. Still taste that perfume on his tongue.

But even more, her sharp gasp as he coldly called her a fool for trusting him rattled in his ears like phantom chains. Her contained expression and shuttered emerald eyes floated across his mind.

Goddamn, he needed an exorcist if he were going to focus or sleep again.

"Cain."

He jerked up his head from his blind study of the report to find the men and women around the table staring at him, including Karina, Achilles and Kenan. He avoided the two men's scrutiny, not just uncomfortable with what he might see in their identical gazes, but with what he might inadvertently reveal to them.

"I'm sorry." He cleared his throat. "I was studying the numbers."

Karina nodded. "I suggested each of us review the proposals and bids then reconvene next week with the top five. And we can narrow it down to three from there."

"Sounds good." Cain tapped the screen and closed the email out. "Is there anything else?" A murmur of noes filled the room, and moments later, the meeting ended, and everyone filed out.

Sighing, Cain followed minutes later. As he headed toward his office, his thoughts again reverted to Devon. What was he going to do? Saturday night, he'd had big intentions of maintaining a safe distance, never crossing that line again. But the past two days had rendered those objectives laughable—and impossible.

He wanted her.

All of the reasons why he should uphold the boundaries he'd placed on this "relationship" remained valid. Now more than ever, since they'd thrown sex into the mix. But that logic took a suicidal leap out the window when up against his memories of that night, the smile of pure joy that had lit her face when she'd seen her family. Or when the brand of her sweet, selfless embrace taunted him with a bone-deep longing he refused to name—was too terrified to name.

No, he couldn't go on much longer like this, he decided, sweeping a glance over his executive assistant's empty chair and desk. He had to make a choice. Either he stick to the facade of a loving fiancé in public and preserve a careful and polite distance in private... Or he surrender to his dark, carnal urges and fuck Devon out of his system.

Pulling open his closed office door, he strode inside, jaw clenched. Only one of those options didn't spell disaster. Only one made sense—

Devon rose from the couch in his sitting area, her emerald eyes slamming into his.

"Cain," she said, her sultry tone soothing the agitation crackling under his skin—and hardening his body to the point of pain. "I'm sorry to show up uninvited, but there was something I needed to speak with you about. Your assistant said I could come in and wait for you..."

She continued speaking, but a dull roar had exploded in his head. And it pounded in his chest, his gut...his cock. Seeing her in the flesh as if she'd been conjured straight out of his dirty fantasies, wearing a black turtleneck dress that clung to every lush curve, all that gorgeous brown-and-gold hair tumbling around her shoulders and playing hide-and-seek with her beautiful breasts...

His will caved, and he buckled under the weight of his lust.

Dropping his files and tablet to the floor, he stalked across the office. With each step, every warning shed from him like dirt knocked off a boot. By the time he stood in front of her, her green eyes were wide with surprise and simmering with heat.

He was not the CEO of Farrell International. Or a

member of one of the oldest, wealthiest families in Boston. He wasn't a son, a brother, not even a bought fiancé.

He was just a man condensed to the basest, most primal parts of himself.

Hunger. Need.

Survival.

Because if he didn't get inside Devon, he would damn sure cease to exist.

Lifting his hands, he cupped her face, tilted it back. His thumbs swept over her high, rounded cheekbones, skimming the tender skin under her amazing eyes.

"Cain," she whispered, her fingers circling his wrists. But she didn't tug him away. Just held on.

His answer was to take. Her mouth. Her gasp. Her breath.

Her.

He molded his lips to hers, dragging his teeth along the soft, damp skin. Smoothing any sting he might've caused with his tongue, then plunging inside her. God, it had been only two days since he'd last savored her, but it might as well have been two weeks, two centuries.

She tasted like sunlight and darkness. Purity and sin.

His salvation, his damnation.

With a growl, he licked and sucked. Thrusted and retreated. Teased and taunted. Worshipped and consumed. He couldn't get enough of her. Of the wet tangle and slide of their tongues. Of her breathy moans and whimpers. Of the restless tightening and loosening of her hands on him.

"What are you willing to give me, Devon?" he asked

against her mouth, repeating the same question he'd posed Saturday night.

Her lashes lifted, revealing her passion-glazed eyes. Her damp lips, already swollen from his kiss, trembled. And the sign of her vulnerability squeezed both his heart and his dick. He pressed a soft kiss to her mouth, nipping lightly, and her ragged inhale rippled over his skin.

"What do you want?" she finally said.

"Everything," he murmured. "I'm a greedy bastard. I want everything."

Her eyes closed, and once more, the sweetness of her breath bathed his mouth, and he tasted her kiss. With a sigh that was part surrender, part need, she loosened her grip on him and slowly sank to her knees.

Shock and a desperate, tearing hunger ripped through him, leaving him in aching, conflicted shreds. Aching, because her hands fumbled with the band on his suit pants, releasing the tab and lowering the zipper. His flesh throbbed, damn near begging to be freed and touched, stroked…swallowed.

Conflicted, because he didn't expect this intimacy from her. Didn't want her to feel pressured to give it to him.

Even though, goddamn, he craved it. Had dreamed about just this.

"Devon, sweetheart." He laid one hand over her hand at his zipper and cradled her cheek with the other. "You don't have to do this." He swept his thumb over her bottom lip, already seeing his cock weighing it down in his mind. Shaking his head, he briefly squeezed his eyes closed, his grip on her hands inadvertently tightening. "Let me—"

"I don't have to do anything," she said, sliding her hand out from under his…and gripping him through his boxer briefs. Stroking. A shiver worked its way through his body, his hips bucking into her grasp. He might come from that alone, that delicate little hand on him. "I *want* to. Are you going to let me, Cain?"

Sometimes, Devon appeared so damn innocent. And then there were other times, like now, when she transformed into a siren capable of luring him to crash against her. To come apart for her.

"Yes, I'm going to let you put your pretty mouth on me," he said, slipping both hands into her hair, tunneling through the thick strands of heavy silk. "Undo me, Devon."

She dipped her hand inside his underwear and cradled his hot, thick flesh. He hissed, his body locking up, going rigid. Pleasure pierced him like a scorching knife, cutting through him, laying him open to her eager touch and the excited glitter in those green eyes. With a low hum that he didn't even think she was aware of releasing, she jerked his boxer briefs lower on his hips, fully exposing him to her hands, gaze and *damn*, her mouth.

That beautiful, sinful tease of a mouth parted, slid over him, taking him inside. So wet. So warm. So *good*. She fisted the lower half of him, pumping while she tormented the top half with her lips and tongue.

"Sweetheart," he rasped, his voice the consistency of freshly churned gravel. "Open wider for me. Please." Yes, he was begging and couldn't care.

She did as he asked, and using his grasp on her head, he held her still and drove into her mouth, his hips rocking forward almost of their own accord. Reaching for the back of her throat on the smooth runway of her tongue. A familiar, but totally new sizzle zipped up his spine, then ran back down as his tip nudged that narrow channel. He groaned, gritting his teeth as she became a lightning rod for the pleasure rippling through him like an electrical current.

"No," he growled to himself, jerking free of her. "Inside." Cupping her under her arms, he yanked her to her feet, trying to be gentle, but undoubtedly failing. "I want to come inside you."

In seconds, he had them on the couch, her panties in his back pocket, her straddled over his thighs and a condom rolled down his erection. Air powered out of his lungs in deep, serrated rasps, and he silently ordered himself to slow down, to not hold her so forcefully. To not bruise her with his barely tempered strength and lust.

Maybe it made him a caveman throwback, but he would take pride in marking her soft, golden skin with their passion. So when she looked at her body the next morning, she would know that for these few stolen moments, she belonged to him. Yeah, he wouldn't mind that. But he didn't want to hurt her. He'd rather cut off his hands first.

She shivered above him, her fingernails biting into him through his suit jacket. This might be the hottest encounter he'd experienced since he'd been introduced to screwing at sixteen. Both of them were still fully clothed, only her glistening sex, thick, gorgeous thighs and his dick were exposed. The redolent musk of their passion perfumed the air, their breath punctuating the silence.

"Are you going to take me in?" he murmured, the strain rippling through his muscles.

Please take me in, Devon.

The plea scraped at the back of his throat, but pride locked it away. Pride and fear of saying too much. Revealing too much.

With their gazes locked, she slowly lowered onto him, her flesh parting, quivering, adjusting...accepting.

Only when she was fully seated on him, squeezing him like a gloved fist, did she lean forward, press her lips to his and whisper, "Yes, Cain. I'll take you in."

A swell of murky emotion —light and dark, joy and pain, need and fear—coalesced in his chest, spinning out until it nearly swallowed him along with the teeth-clenching pleasure. Deliberately, he shoved everything down—everything but the pleasure. He let it bend him, consume him, as she slid up his dick, those tiny feminine muscles fluttering around him. He didn't move, handing over full control, but his fingers dented her hips with the effort of not slamming her back down. And goddamn, did she reward him for holding off. She gifted him with an equally slow and torturous glide back down, dragging a long groan—hell, a stone's throw from a whimper—out of him.

"Again, sweetheart," he grunted. "I need more." God, did she give him more.

She rode him.

Fucked him.

Broke him.

Her breathless cries and dirty moans stroked his flesh. But with each roll of her hips, each pulse around him and over him, she shoved him closer and closer to release. He held on like a man hanging on to a crumbling cliff by his fingernails.

"Touch me," Devon croaked against his neck. "Please touch me."

He understood her pained request even as her channel spasmed around him. Reaching between them, he rubbed his thumb once, twice, three times over the stiff button of nerves at the top of her sex. Her body clamped down on him, seizing him in a strangling embrace.

As she came undone, quivering and sucking him impossibly deeper, he gripped her tight, held her aloft and pounded inside her, chasing the perfection that loomed so close. Pleasure arced through him in fire-hot, blazing strikes. They struck his spine, his lower back, the soles of his feet, his dick.

Devon took his thrusts, her arms wrapped around his shoulders, her teeth sinking into the base of his throat. And it was that bite, the erotic sting of it, her marking of him, that sent him cracking wide down the middle. Thank God for the soundproofing of his office, because his hoarse shout rebounded off the walls, echoing in his head.

And even as he let go of his passion, his control, he held on to her.

Fifteen

Devon hovered on the bottom step of the grand staircase that spiraled far above her. The light purple and gray of the day's dying light streamed into the equally grand foyer of the Beacon Hill mansion. Part of her wanted nothing more than to jog back up the steps, head back down the hall to the room she'd just exited and climb back into the big bed with the tangled covers and sheets.

Cain's bed. Cain's sheets.

But they were both responsible for tangling them.

A shaky breath escaped her, and she pressed her palm to her fluttering stomach. Silly, considering all that she'd been doing with him since they left Farrell International hours ago. Heat crawled up her throat and poured into her face when she recalled how she'd fallen to her knees for him, let him fill her mouth and then her body *in his office*.

Again, silly she should be embarrassed given what she'd been allowing him to do to her since—and what she'd done to him in return. But when it came to Cain Farrell, nothing made sense. Not her decisions. Not her logic. Not her lack of control. Not this magnetic, almost *desperate* pull toward him.

She'd gone to Farrell to broach the subject of his real estate deal. Shame slithered through her. Yes, she'd had every intention of lobbying on her father's behalf. And when Cain's assistant had allowed her to wait in his empty office, she'd stared at his desk, so close to skirting around it and searching the massive piece of furniture and his computer for anything regarding the project. Ultimately though, she couldn't sink quite *that* low.

But when Cain stalked into the cavernous room, all thoughts about real estate and her father bolted from her head. Not two nights earlier, she'd vowed not to be vulnerable with Cain again. But it'd been the glimmer of confusion and need in his blue-gray gaze—the same emotions so rife inside her—that had spurred her surrender to him, his kiss, his touch. Even knowing it would lead to only more problems, more mistakes.

And here she stood, in Cain's house, tumbling deeper and deeper into the quagmire that was their "relationship."

"What are you doing down here?" Cain appeared before her, his powerful chest bare, wearing only a black pair of lounging pants that clung to his narrow hips like a jealous lover. "I was going to bring food up to you." His gaze surveyed her from the unruly, freshly sexed hair, over his white dress shirt that she'd slipped on and down to her painted toes. She fidgeted, aware that she'd become *that* woman—the one who wore her man's clothes just to be closer to him, to be surrounded by his scent.

Only Cain wasn't her man. Not truly.

"Are you hungry?"

The simmer of heat brightening his eyes kindled the same embers of desire in her. Beneath the fine cotton, her nipples beaded and the flesh between her legs softened, swelled. She opened her mouth, about to tell him "not for food," when her stomach growled. Loudly.

For the first time, a real, full-fledged smile curved his mouth, the amusement reflected in his gaze. Her breath snagged in her lungs at the beauty of it. She marveled that it was directed at her.

"Come on." He clasped her hand in his and guided her off the last step. "It's not much given my culinary skills, but it should be enough to suppress the rebellion." His chin dipped toward her stomach.

In spite of the flush transforming her face into a fire hazard, she laughed and followed him to the kitchen.

Contrary to his assertion of "not much," the spread of cold cuts, cheeses, bread, vegetables and fruit impressed her. They fixed thick sandwiches and settled at the table in the surprisingly cozy nook to dine.

Surreal. It seemed so surreal that she sat with Cain like any ordinary couple eating homemade deli sandwiches. He asked about her family, and she told him about spending time with them before they left, which led to childhood stories. They laughed together, and *God*, the sound of that low, deep timbre shouldn't cause her belly to bottom out or her heart to seize and beat in triple time.

Oh no.

This didn't bode well for her. At all. But she didn't get up and leave. Instead, she stayed and savored every moment. Hoarding it away.

Later, Cain gathered their dishes and carried them to the sink. On bare feet, she rose from her chair and padded to the huge bay windows that covered the back wall. Though night had fully chased away dusk, soft light from gas lampposts provided a shadowed view of the garden where they'd met weeks ago. Funny how such a serendipitous meeting would lead them here.

Well, that meeting, her father and his damn contract.

Not going to think about him. Not now. Not here.

"It's so beautiful," she murmured, lifting a hand, fingers splayed and hovering over the pristine glass. As if she could reach right through it and touch the carefully tended hedges and flowers.

"It was my mother's," Cain said quietly. She started, not having heard him come up behind her. But his reflection towered over her in the glass mirroring their images. "It was the only change my father allowed her to make to the house that's been in his family for generations. Even now, I don't know why he did. Maybe because it added to the property value," he mused, his voice and the accompanying chuckle bearing a bitter note.

The question that had been nagging her since they'd

arrived at his house Saturday night danced on her tongue. And not for the first time. She'd quelled the urge to ask on those previous occasions, but tonight... With the walls they'd both erected to protect themselves a little more nebulous, she risked it.

"Why do you hate this house so much?" she whispered to his reflection.

Silence met her, and inwardly, she winced, regretting the impulse to intrude on his past. Damn her and her curiosity.

"I'm sorry. I shouldn't have—"

"My father abused me when I was younger. This house was my prison and personal hell."

Horror and a wailing grief welled inside her, and she whimpered at the pain. She tried to whirl around, to wrap her arms around him, but two big hands on her shoulders prevented the movement. Cain didn't let her turn around, but kept her facing forward, his chest pressed to her back. She ached to hold him, but this wasn't about her.

However he needed to get through his story, she would respect it.

"Barron was never an affectionate man. He ran our family the same way he did the company—in total control, calculating, manipulative and ruthless. If not for my mother, there wouldn't have been any love or warmth in this house. But he started beating me when I turned seven, and even her love couldn't protect me. He called it 'making a man out of me.' All I understood was there must've been something so defective, so horrible about me that he would backhand me as soon as talk to me. But as bad as the physical abuse was, the emotional and mental violence was worse. Never knowing what awaited me when I came home from school or when he arrived from work. Trying to be perfect, when no matter how hard I tried, I could never achieve it. Suffering from stomachaches and headaches from the stress. Throwing up whenever he summoned me to the library. Because I knew what awaited me there. And nobody could stop him. Nobody could save me," he murmured.

Devon closed her eyes, biting her lip to hold back the tears stinging her eyes. She hated Barron Farrell in this moment. Detested him for hurting his son. For putting that distant note in the voice of the man the boy had become. As if retelling this story pained him so much he had to speak as if it had happened to someone else.

Oh yes. She hated Barron.

"Did he abuse your mother, too?" she whispered.

"Not physically, no. But he cheated and flaunted his infidelities in her face. Belittled her, called her names… I often wondered why he bothered to marry and have children, and the only reason I can come up with is he wanted victims to torture. My mother could've left, could've divorced him. But that would've meant leaving me behind because there was no way Barron would've let her have custody. So she stayed until I was old enough to defend myself. Not long after I graduated college and moved out of this house, she divorced my father, and I never returned here. Until the funeral."

No wonder he'd been in that garden. Having to return to this hellish place… She frowned at their reflections.

"Why stay here then? It's obvious to me that you can't stand stepping foot in here."

"Because it's another stipulation of my father's will," he explained. "I have to live here for a year or risk losing Farrell International."

"That bastard," she hissed, fury a living thing inside her. "It wasn't enough that he tortured you as a child, but he's still trying to manipulate you from the grave." She shook her head. "After the year is up, you should turn this place into a home for women and children who are victims of domestic violence. Give them a place to transition between a shelter and being on their own. That would show him from wherever he is now... And just for the record, I don't think he's looking *down* on us," she muttered.

His low laughter rumbled against her back and he rubbed his chin over the top of her head. The casual display of affection had longing for what could never be lodging in her throat. The reminder sent splinters of pain digging beneath her skin. Especially in light of what he'd just revealed.

"I'm sorry for all you suffered, Cain," she said softly, covering the hand on her shoulder, threading their fingers together. "That man has stolen so much from you. Your childhood. Your innocence. Your brothers. And you didn't deserve any of that. I can't imagine..." She shook her head, her grasp on him tightening. "The man you've become now is a testimony to the character and strength your father had no hope of ever possessing. Then, after spending years choiceless and powerless, my father comes along and tries to strip both from you again. I'm so sorry," she rasped, now fully comprehending why Cain hated her father—and her—so much. He'd survived his horror of a childhood, claimed his power and control, and then they came along to remind him of the hell he'd endured.

Spinning around, she faced him, forced herself to meet the scalpel-like gaze that seemed to peer to the very soul of her.

"I have something to tell you."

Her father had warned her not to reveal the truth to Cain, but given what he'd just confessed, there was no way she could continue deceiving him. She owed him the truth.

"You asked me why I didn't walk away from this deal between our fathers." His eyes narrowed slightly, but she inhaled a deep breath and continued before losing her nerve. "He threatened the community center. If I didn't go through with the engagement and marriage, he wouldn't just have me fired, but would revoke his financial support and convince other much needed donors to do the same. I didn't care so much about my job, but too many other people depend on the center. I couldn't tell you before now because Dad…" She trailed off, shrugged. "Anyway, I thought you should know—"

He cupped her face, cutting off the flow of words. His mouth slanted over hers, voracious and demanding. With a moan, she tilted her head back, opening wider for the erotic onslaught, circling her arms around him and clutching his back for purchase.

His hands fell away from her cheeks, and bending his knees, he grasped the backs of her thighs and hiked her high in the air. Instinctively, she wrapped her legs around his waist, shifting her arms to his neck. And when he laid her out on the kitchen table like a meal he couldn't wait to devour, she surrendered to his passion. To the need that his kiss had ignited in her.

But even as he removed his shirt from her and drew her nipple into his mouth, she couldn't silence the voice that whispered Cain would never be able to see past her father's sins to love her.

Which presented one hell of a problem.

Because she'd fallen in love with him.

Sixteen

"Cain," Ben called from the doorway of the study.

Cain glanced up from gathering files to bring to the office. The office he was late going in to. The minutes ticked closer and closer to ten, and he had an eleven-thirty meeting. Usually, he arrived at Farrell before anyone else except the security guards, but not this morning. And he couldn't complain. Not when the reason for him being late had just slipped from his bed a few hours earlier.

A smile tugged at his mouth as heat slid through him. There'd been a time when he would've never allowed a woman to interfere with his business life. But with Devon? The woman had thrown him curveballs from the moment they met. And he couldn't regret running a little late if it meant waking up curled around her curvy little body, her scent in his nose and his sheets.

Especially considering her confession the night before.

It shouldn't have surprised him that Gregory Cole would blackmail his own daughter, but it had. The man had no lows to which he wouldn't sink. And though hearing her admission sickened Cain, it'd also hauled a huge weight off his chest. Until it lifted, he hadn't realized just how much her supposed complicity with her father had eaten at him. The relief and emotional intensity from unloading his own past on her had triggered a lust that he'd worked out on the kitchen table. Another unprecedented event for him.

A contradiction of emotions had warred within him as he'd dropped her off at her home that morning. An almost overwhelming need to call her back, to stay another day in bed, locked away from the demands of the world. And a sense of...fear.

Because at some point, Devon had infiltrated his carefully constructed guard and become important.

And yeah, that was terrifying.

He still couldn't fully trust her.

Maybe it was because of all he'd suffered as a child or who her father was, but he had a difficult time letting anyone close. Her. Kenan and Achilles. Even his mother, to a degree. Yet, none of them threatened his cocoon of self-preservation, his equilibrium, his control.

Not like Devon.

"Cain," Ben said again.

He shook his head, shooting his butler an apologetic smile. "I'm sorry, Ben. Yes?"

"There's a Gregory Cole here. He said you would see him even though he showed up uninvited."

That fast, anger kindled. Damn, the balls on this man. "Send him in."

Ben nodded and ducked out. Moments later, Gregory strode in, and it required every bit of Cain's control to remain behind the desk. His father and Gregory were two of a kind, and just being in the same room had Cain itching to take another shower. After he slammed him against the wall.

"What are you doing here, Cole?" Cain asked, voice cold and impatient. "Showing up where you're not wanted or invited is becoming a bad habit for you."

The man's smile remained in place although his green eyes glinted with irritation. "Considering we're soon to be family, we shouldn't stand on formality," Gregory said. He gestured to one of the chairs in front of Cain's desk. "May I sit?"

"No," Cain clipped out. "I'm headed into the office. So whatever you came here to say, you need to make it quick."

"Fine." Gregory tugged at his cuff, the movement stiff. "I heard about the North Station project Farrell International is heading. I want in as an investor."

Cain blinked. Stared at the other man. Then barked out a disbelieving laugh. "You're joking." When Gregory's mouth hardened, his shoulders going rigid underneath his flawlessly tailored jacket, Cain laughed again. "You're not joking." He shook his head. "I can't trust you, but you think I would do business with you? Ask my partners to trust you?"

"My firm is above reproach—"

"No," Cain interrupted, voice flat. "And if you still don't understand that. Hell no. Now—" he stuffed folders into his leather case "—if that's all you came over here for..."

"I didn't want to go here, but if Devon had convinced you as I asked her to, then this wouldn't be necessary." Gregory tsked, mock regret coloring his voice.

Unease crept into Cain's chest, clenching his gut.

If Devon had convinced him as he'd asked?

"What are you talking about?"

"If Devon had used her influence, then I wouldn't have to once more use the...information I have to convince you to let me in on this project. But here we are." Gregory spread his hands wide, palms up. "Now, I can come to your office later to talk details."

Rage, fueled by betrayal, rushed swift and hot through him. Rage at Gregory extorting him again. Proving that Cain would never be out from under this man's thumb. Cain would forever be at his mercy as long as he possessed that inflammatory material on his mother. And Devon... She'd known all along about her father's intentions to infiltrate this project. And she'd said *nothing*. All the time they'd spent together, she could've but hadn't. The sting of that betrayal burrowed deep, past skin and bone to the part of him he'd vowed no one would ever hurt again.

Giving in again wasn't an option. He'd already done it once, and it landed him here—a fish caught on a never-ending hook. But, dammit. How could he get out of this? What was his next move?

His mind raced with a possible solution. Anything that would free him from this man and his deceitful daughter. One thing he treasured above all was loyalty. And feeling safe with a person. She'd betrayed both. Maybe he didn't have a way of escape now, but by God, he would find one.

"So what's your decision, Cain?" Gregory pressed. The smug smile on his face telegraphed his confidence that he'd won Cain's cooperation.

Well, he could go screw himself.

"The answer is not a chance in hell," he ground out, glaring at Gregory. Anger, pain and disillusionment poisoned his blood. "It isn't enough to force your daughter on me. Now you want to force your way into my family business as well."

"I certainly have no intention of being forced on anyone."

Pain blazed a white-hot path through her, and for a moment, she could barely breathe past it. But she forced her feet forward, entering Cain's study and approaching her father and the man she'd just admitted to loving the night before.

The man who had just made it infinitely clear that he wanted nothing to do with her.

Oh God, that hurt.

Forcing a calm to her expression that was a complete lie, she stopped in front of Cain's desk and dropped the thick manila folder in her hand on top.

"Devon," her father snapped. "What are you doing here?"

"Setting everything right," she replied. "I hate to break it to you, Dad, but the engagement—if you could ever really call it that—is done. I'm calling it off."

"What?" he demanded, stalking to her side. "What are you talking about, girl?"

She didn't reply to her father, nor did she remove her gaze from Cain's. His eyes simmered with anger, and her heart constricted, pain flaring in her chest. She'd overheard his conversation with her father. Knew what he thought. Even after last night. He still believed her capable of betraying him. She would never be trustworthy in his eyes. Would always be the burden he'd just called her.

Well, she was no one's burden, no one's liability.

Not anymore.

"Take it," she whispered, nudging it closer with a fingertip. "You're free. And so am I."

"Devon." Her father gripped her arm and turned her to face him. Crimson slashed across his cheekbones, fury and worry warring for dominance in his eyes. "What did you do?"

"What I should've done when you first started all of this, Dad. After you left for work this morning, I opened your safe," she murmured, regret a heavy weight on her shoulders. "It didn't take me long to figure out the combination." She huffed out a humorless laugh. "Mom's birthday. Seems almost sacrilegious to use anything about her in relation to what you've done. But I found everything you had on Cain's mother. It's in that file."

She waved a hand toward Cain's desk. "I have to be honest. I didn't expect either of you to be here. I intended to just leave this here for you, Cain, and talk to you later, Dad. But since you both are, we can get this over with now. Two birds with one stone, and all that. It's done. This is all finished."

"How could you?" Gregory yelled, dropping his hand and stepping away from her as if she disgusted him. "I'm your father, and you betray me like this? For a man who doesn't even want anything to do with you?"

She took that truthful jab, absorbed it and pushed on. "You betrayed me first," she shot back, straightening her shoulders and hiking her chin. "I've been nothing but a puppet to you. A pawn to move around on your chessboard. I'm through, Dad. I'm your daughter. And it's all I've wanted to be for a very, very long time. But if you can't be my father—the father who loved and accepted me, who thought I was perfect even when I clearly wasn't, who thought the sun rose and fell on me simply because he loved me—then we can't have a relationship anymore. I'll love you from a distance rather than be involved in a toxicity that drains me of my self-worth and confidence."

"You're no daughter of mine," her father stated, the ice in his voice piercing her clean through, and then he pivoted on his heel and stormed out.

She absorbed that verbal blow, too.

"Devon," Cain said, and she returned her attention to him, holding up a hand, palm out.

"No. Both you and my father have said more than enough," she said, referring to the conversation she overheard. "For too long, I've passively allowed myself to go along with the men in my life. To be toyed with and maneuvered like a plaything. I'm done. There was a time I loved a man who didn't love me in return, who used me. You might not want an 'in' like Donald did, but I won't be your surrogate for venting your anger. I've never betrayed you. Never hurt you. I've only…"

Loved you.

But she held back those words. No, he couldn't have that from her. Her heart might be shattering because of how much he filled it to breaking, but when she walked out of here, it would be with her pride. He couldn't have that either.

"I'm through paying for someone else's sins. I've been paying the price with my father for my mother dying and leaving him. I've paid the price for being too blind to see when a man wanted my father's favor more than he wanted me. And with you, I'm paying for being his daughter. You've never seen me as more than that, Cain. And initially, I couldn't blame you. But after getting to know me… After spending time with me… After being in me…" Her voice cracked on the reminder of how tender and loving he'd been with her, and how it'd all been a lie. "You once asked me who I really was. I hoped you would come to see that, know me for myself. But you never will. I will always be a reminder of the man who blackmailed you and threatened your mother. I'm so much more than that. And I'm tired of trying to prove it to you."

"Devon," Cain murmured, and for the first time his

gaze softened, losing the edge that had been there since she'd intruded into the study. "I know who you are."

"Too late," she whispered, loving him and resenting him for saying that to her now. "I don't believe you. I saw your face, your eyes when I walked in here. You thought I had sided with my father. The truth is he did ask me to approach you about that deal. He even instructed me to steal the info on it. But I couldn't do that to you. And had I known he would attempt to blackmail you again, I would've told you about his desire to be in on the project. That's my mistake—a mistake. The truth is, Cain, you can never trust me."

He didn't contradict her, which proved her wrong. She *could* hurt worse.

"I've been down this road before, Cain. I'll put it in terms you might understand better. I've invested all of myself into a man I loved who couldn't give me the same in return. I'd rather be alone, giving one hundred percent to myself, than receiving fifty from someone else. I'm worth one hundred. I deserve it."

She stared at him for a moment longer, soaked in every feature of his beautiful, hard face because it might be the last time. Then she turned and left.

Without looking back.

Seventeen

A hard rap reverberated on the study door, but before he could growl for Ben to go away, the door swung open. Kenan and Achilles strode in.

Dammit.

Cain ground his teeth together and he leaned back in his office chair, not uttering a word as the two men approached the desk. It'd been three days since he'd been to the office—three days since his confrontation with Gregory Cole and Devon.

Devon.

Jesus, just the echo of her name in his head had him wanting to reach for the bottle of Scotch. Drinking himself into oblivion had temporarily helped him forget the dagger-sharp agony Devon's words had sliced into him. But he could only down so much liquor. And after he'd crawled into the shower and dressed the next morning, he'd locked himself in the study, replacing Scotch with work. He could've gone in to the office—it would've made sense to escape the scene of the crime, so to speak. Call it punishment, but he remained in here, where the echoes of her remained to torment him, castigate him for the wrongs he'd committed.

I've been down this road before, Cain... I've invested all of myself into a man I loved who couldn't give me the same in return.

He briefly squeezed his eyes shut, but the action couldn't purge the impassioned statement from his head. He'd been analyzing it over and over like there was a puzzle buried in those words. She'd obviously been hurt before but could she possibly love…?

He shook his head. No, she didn't. And there was no point in even considering it.

"So this is where you've been hiding yourself," Kenan said, dropping into one of the visitors chairs in front of his desk. Achilles took up his post across from them, propping a shoulder against the wall. "We were trying to be patient and give you time to get over your Heathcliff impersonation, but apparently, you need a kick in the ass."

Cain snorted. "Heathcliff?"

"What?" Kenan shrugged. "I read."

"You look like shit," Achilles rumbled, and the blunt assessment had Cain's spine snapping straight.

"I didn't ask either of you for your opinion or to come over here. What do you want? Shouldn't you be at work?" he growled.

Kenan arched an eyebrow. "Shouldn't you? I thought you'd be too worried to leave the bastard Farrells at the office without your careful supervision." He tsked. "Falling down on the job, Cain."

"Are you trying to piss me off? Because it's working," Cain said, not bothering to keep the menace out of his voice.

"Good," Achilles grunted. "Then maybe you can get that stick out of your ass about every-fucking-thing and stop treating us like the enemy. We want to be here as much as you want us here."

"I doubt that," Cain snapped. "You two think you're doing me a favor by staying here, because you have to give up a year of your life? Try thirty-two. Thirty-two years of hell living, working with and suffering at the hands of a cold, manipulative, vicious bastard. Yes, I want you here. Would've begged you to stay here because everything I endured with that man had to mean something."

The words exploded from him in an ugly, bitter torrent that he couldn't stop. Kenan stared at him, and Achilles slowly pushed away from the wall, straightening.

"What does that mean, Cain?" Achilles growled.

Unlike the previous times, the truth burned a trail up his throat, and he didn't hold it back. Couldn't. Didn't want to. Not anymore.

He told them everything—about his childhood with their father, the abuse, even about Gregory Cole's blackmail and his relationship with Devon. Through it all, Kenan and Achilles remained silent, not asking questions, just allowing Cain to purge his soul in a way he hadn't even done with Devon. When he finished, his breath grated against his throat, and the labored sound echoed in the quiet room.

Achilles moved toward him in his oddly graceful gait, and in moments, he'd pulled Cain into his arms, holding him tight. It should've been weird, being embraced by this giant, but no. It was…family. Tears burned his eyes as the burden of anger and bitterness that he'd borne since the reading of that damn will crumbled and fell. And for the first time since they all met in this house, he could call this man brother.

"I'm sorry, Cain," Achilles muttered in his ear. "I'm sorry you had to suffer that shit. None of us should."

The curious choice of words struck Cain, and he suspected that maybe his younger brother could more than sympathize with him about being on the end of an abusive person.

Achilles neither confirmed nor denied anything, but released Cain with a squeeze of his shoulder.

"Now I want to dig the bastard up, kill him and then bury him all over again," Kenan spat, standing in front of the desk. He shook his head, his blue-gray eyes shadowed. "I'm sorry, Cain. About everything." A muscle ticked along his jaw, and his mouth hardened. "I knew something was off about Gregory Cole. And I'm not going to lie, I had my suspicions about the relationship with Devon. But you only need to be around her for five minutes to realize she's not like her father. She proved that by going against him to give you the material on your mother." His voice lowered but didn't lose the adamant edge. "I know we haven't been in each other's lives for very long, but you are my brother. And so I'm going to tell you this—you fucked up by letting her walk away."

"I didn't *let* her walk away," Cain insisted. "And she was right about one thing. I don't know if I could trust her. I don't know…" How to explain that his greatest fear wasn't losing the company. It wasn't even leaving his mother exposed to Gregory's extortion.

It was letting someone in, loving them, and being hurt by them.

It was opening his heart and being deemed unworthy… unlovable. That fear had kept him from committing to anyone or anything except his job. Because the work, the company, he could control. Other people? Their hearts? Hell, his own heart? No.

"If you can't trust her, then who?" Achilles insisted. "I get it, Cain." In his eyes, identical to Cain's, he again saw the shadows that deepened his suspicion about his brother's past. "But you deserve happiness if any of us do. And she's it for you. I don't care how this started, we saw how she looked at you…and how you looked at her. Don't continue letting your father control and manipulate you from the grave."

That man has stolen so much from you. Your child-hood. Your innocence. Your brothers.

Achilles, Kenan, Devon… They were right. Barron had stolen so much more than his childhood. He'd robbed Cain of his ability to believe in the innate goodness in people. If the man who was supposed to love and protect him had hurt him so deeply, had destroyed his trust, how could he have faith in, depend on, others?

He couldn't. He could only trust himself.

But not with Devon.

From that first meeting in his mother's garden, she'd shown him compassion, kindness, humor, given him comfort. Him, a stranger to her at the time.

He'd asked who she really was. The shy, funny woman from the garden? The loyal daughter? The gentle, loving youth coordinator? The passionate lover?

His answer: all of them.

And he loved each one.

God, did he love her.

Maybe he had from the moment she admitted to wondering about the color of his eyes. Or when she'd called out everyone in that god-awful party for being ghoulish when he'd needed comfort.

The exact second didn't matter. What did was that he'd allowed her to leave him without any intention of brightening his life again.

"I fucked up," he whispered.

"Yeah, you did," Achilles agreed, nodding.

"But luckily you have something on your side now that you didn't before," Kenan announced.

Cain frowned. "What?"

Kenan spread his arms wide. "Me," he scoffed.

Achilles snorted, and Cain laughed. An honest-to-God, full-belly laugh from a place that had been locked up tight for so long.

He felt good. He felt…free.

He had his brothers.

Now he had to go find the woman he loved and convince her to give him another chance.

He had nothing to lose, and the world to gain.

Because Devon was his world.

Eighteen

Devon sighed as she entered the lobby of the community center. A fatigued but good sigh. It'd been a long day, but she loved those. Especially now. They tired her out, didn't leave her time to think. And by the time she arrived home—home now being her apartment in Charlestown—she ate whatever takeout she picked up and dropped into bed.

For the first time, she was on her own—no, that wasn't true. The past weekend, she'd driven the five hours to New Jersey to spend the weekend with her family. It'd been like stepping back into the past when everything had been innocent and happy. Being with her aunts, uncles and cousins had been a balm to her battered soul. The only hairy moment had been when her aunt had asked about Cain and her father. She'd been so tempted to unload everything. But in the end, she'd just said they were both fine and left it at that. As selfish and, hell, criminal, as her father had been, she didn't want to tarnish his image in his brothers' and sisters' eyes.

She might have walked out of all of this with a broken heart and a permanent rift with her father, but at least she had her family back. She called that a win.

Even if she stared at the ceiling for hours with burning eyes before falling to sleep from sheer exhaustion. Only to dream about a beautiful man with wolf eyes.

It'd been a week since she'd last seen Cain. Time. That's all she needed to get over him. And she would. One day.

"Finally leaving for the evening, Devon?" Harry, the security guard on duty, called out to her.

She smiled at the older man. "Finally," she said. "And there's a Netflix binge with my name on it."

He laughed. "My wife just watched that show starring the Superman guy. Except he has white hair like that elf from *The Lord of the Rings*. She loved it. A little too much, if you ask me."

Devon grinned. "Tell her she has great taste." Waving goodbye, she exited the building, headed down the sidewalk toward the small parking lot. Tomorrow started the basketball tournament so she would need to arrive early to—

"Devon."

She swallowed down a yelp and raised her fist, keys poking out between her fingers. But then she saw the man pushing off the brick building and taking steps in her direction.

Shock ricocheted through her, and she couldn't move. Couldn't do anything but stare at Cain as he approached her. Against her will, she scanned the starkly beautiful lines of his face. Met the gaze that never failed to send her pulse pounding. Her fingers itched to stroke the full, sensual mouth and the rock-hard line of his jaw. She curled those traitorous fingers into her palm.

"Cain," she rasped. Paused, and cleared her throat. "What are you doing here?"

He slid his hands in his front pockets, the action stretching his shirt over his wide chest. God, she tried not to notice. "I'm here for you."

Not "to see you." But "for you."

What did that mean?

Didn't matter. She didn't care—*couldn't* care.

"You need to go," she said, injecting steel into her voice that she fought to feel. But with him standing there in front of her, the resolve not to touch him, not to get within five feet of him wavered. *He hurt you, dammit*, she hissed at her wayward, glutton-for-punishment heart. And as much as she longed to curl up against his chest, she refused to settle for scraps of his affection or love. "Really, just leave."

"Devon," he said, and after a brief hesitation, shifted forward. Under the light of the streetlamp, she caught the faint shadows under his eyes. They reminded her of how she looked in the morning after a sleepless night, before she applied concealer. "I don't have the right to ask this but please, hear me out. And if you still want me to walk away and never bother you again, I will."

It was the "please" that gave her pause. A man like Cain didn't say it often. With a jerk of her chin, she nodded. But instead of talking, he lowered his head, studying the sidewalk. Finally, he released a soft, self-deprecating chuckle.

"I had what I wanted to say all planned out. It was going to be simple and straight to the point. Kenan has connections at Boston University and wanted me to come here with the marching band." He lifted his head, and surprise rippled through her again at the sight of the true smile curving his mouth. As did the casual mention of his half brother. "But I turned him down. Even if they were going to play 'I Will Always Love You.'" She rocked back at that admission, her lips parting on a wheeze of breath, but Cain continued. "I don't need gimmicks to tell you I'm sorry. I'm so damn ashamed of how I treated you. It was unfair, assigning someone else's sins to you. I, more than anyone, understand we're not our parents. And you..." He huffed out a breath, his voice taking on a reverent tone that belonged to works of art, to prayers, not her. Especially not from him.

But it was there. For her.

"You're the best of all of us. Beautiful. Kind. Selfless. So damn brave it terrifies and shames me. Loyal. And *mine*."

She stumbled back a step, rocked by that impassioned claim. Self-preservation made a last-ditch effort to save her from herself, and she raised her arm, palm out. "Stop. I don't want to hear any more. I can't..."

But Cain didn't listen to her. He strode forward until her hand pressed to his chest. And dammit, her fingers rebelled again by curling into the dense muscle. He covered her hand with his bigger one, holding her to him.

"You were right, Devon. You deserve one hundred percent of a person. Their fidelity, their security, their protection, their passion, their heart. Their soul. And, sweetheart, you have all of that from me. You've owned me for so long, but I was too afraid to let you in, to risk you seeing the real me and deciding I wasn't worthy enough. I was afraid to trust that my heart was held by the gentlest of hands—that it had found its home. *You own me, Devon*," he repeated on a jagged whisper. "And maybe because of how I've hurt you, I'm not worthy of you, but I promise I won't stop trying to be. You are worth the fight. Because I love you."

Her body jerked as those three words jolted through her like an electrical current.

Her mind rebelled even as her heart nearly leaped out of her chest to throw itself at him. He couldn't love her. He couldn't because she wanted him to—so damn much. She wasn't aware of shaking her head until he nodded.

"Yes, I do. I love you, Devon." He lifted the hand not holding hers captive and stroked his fingers down her cheek. Then he reached into his pants pocket and withdrew a small gold key. He extended it toward her.

"What is this?" She accepted it but didn't remove her gaze from his.

"It's the key to a safety-deposit box containing all the information on my mother that you took from your father's safe. I'm handing it back to you. There's no one else I trust more to keep it safe. To protect not just me, but my family. You're not your father, Devon, and I'll never look at you and see him. I only see the woman I trust and love beyond reason or explanation."

Her fingers curled around the key, pressing it to her heart. The heart that wholly belonged to him.

"I love you," she whispered. "I love you so much."

She removed her hand from his chest to throw both her arms around him and hold on. And she would never let go. She was his, and he was all hers.

"Sweetheart." He cupped her chin and tilted her head back, brushing his lips over her temple, her cheek, her nose and finally, her mouth. "Say it again."

"I love you. I love you. I love you," she chanted, then laughing, threw her head back and shouted to the sky, "I love you."

Chuckling, he buried his face against her throat, his words muffled, but she didn't need to hear him to know he whispered a vow of love. Of forever.

"One thing," she said. Cain lifted his head, cradling her face in both of his palms.

"Anything."

"Next time you come groveling—because given who we are, I'm pretty sure there will be a next time—I want the marching band."

His bark of laughter echoed in the air, and hers joined in. She reveled in that sound of joy, savored it, knowing it was just the first of many for them.

"Come home with me," he murmured. "Come make new memories with me and exorcise the old ones."

"Yes," she replied without hesitation, placing a soft, tender kiss to his lips. She stared into his wolf eyes and basked under the love gleaming there for her. "New memories. And tomorrow—" she held up the key "—we have a fire to build."

"I think that will be our first real date," he teased, sweeping his thumb over her bottom lip. "I can't wait."

And as he lowered his head and took her mouth again, she couldn't wait either.

For tonight.

For the date.

For their forever.

* * * * *

When Achilles Farrell indulges in a sizzling one-night stand, the woman he never expected to see again ends up working for his company! Now, he has to keep his hands off. But the passion between them still burns hot as ever...

Achilles's story is coming in August 2021!

Until then, enjoy the Blackout Billionaires from USA TODAY *bestselling author Naima Simone!*

The Billionaire's Bargain
Black Tie Billionaire
Blame It on the Billionaire

WE HOPE YOU ENJOYED
THIS BOOK FROM

HARLEQUIN
DESIRE

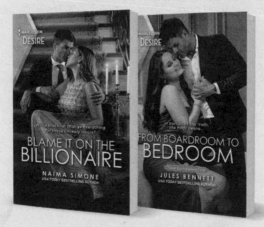

*Luxury, scandal, desire—welcome to
the lives of the American elite.*

Be transported to the worlds of oil barons, family dynasties,
moguls and celebrities. Get ready for juicy plot twists,
delicious sensuality and intriguing scandal.

6 NEW BOOKS AVAILABLE EVERY MONTH!

#2773 THE WIFE HE NEEDS

Westmoreland Legacy: The Outlaws • by Brenda Jackson
Looking to settle down, Alaskan CEO Garth Outlaw thinks he wants
a convenient bride. What he doesn't know is that his pilot,
Regan Fairchild, wants *him*. Now, with two accidental weeks together in
paradise, will the wife he needs be closer than he realized?

#2774 TEMPTED BY THE BOSS

Texas Cattleman's Club: Rags to Riches • by Jules Bennett
The only way to get Kelly Prentiss's irresistible workaholic boss
Luke Holloway to relax is to trick him—into taking a vacation with her!
The island heat ignites a passion they can't ignore, but will it be back to
business once their getaway ends?

#2775 OFF LIMITS ATTRACTION

The Heirs of Hansol • by Jayci Lee
Ambitious Colin Song wants his revenge—by working with producer
Jihae Park. But remaining enemies is a losing battle with their sizzling
chemistry! Yet how can they have a picture-perfect ending when
everyone's secret motives come to light?

#2776 HOT HOLIDAY FLING

by Joss Wood
Burned before, the only thing businessman Hunt Sheridan wants is
a no-strings affair with career-focused Adie Ashby-Tate. When he
suggests a Christmas fling, it's an offer she can't refuse. But will their hot
holiday fantasy turn into a gift neither was expecting?

#2777 SEDUCING THE LOST HEIR

Clashing Birthrights • by Yvonne Lindsay
When identical twin Logan Harper learns he was stolen at birth, he vows
to claim the life he was denied. Until he's mistakenly seduced by
Honor Gould, *his twin's fiancée*! Their connection is undeniable, but
they're determined not to make the same mistake twice...

#2778 TAKING ON THE BILLIONAIRE

Redhawk Reunion • by Robin Covington
Tess Lynch once helped billionaire Adam Redhawk find his Cherokee
family. Now he needs her again to find who's sabotaging his company.
But she has a secret agenda that doesn't stop sparks from flying. Will
the woman he can't resist be his downfall?

*Looking to settle down, Alaskan CEO Garth Outlaw
thinks he wants a convenient bride. What he doesn't
know is that his pilot, Regan Fairchild, wants him. Now,
with two accidental weeks together in paradise, will the
wife he needs be closer than he realized?*

Read on for a sneak peek at
The Wife He Needs
by New York Times *bestselling author Brenda Jackson.*

"May I go on record to make something clear, Regan?" Garth
asked, kicking off his shoes.

She swallowed. He was standing, all six feet and three inches
of him, at the foot of the bed, staring at her with the same intensity
that she felt. She wasn't sure what he had to say, but she definitely
wanted to hear it.

"Yes," she said in an almost whisper.

"You don't need me to make you feel sexy, desired and wanted.
You are those things already. What I intend to do is to make you feel
needed," he said, stepping away from the bed to pull his T-shirt over
his head and toss it on a nearby chair. "If you only knew the depth
of my need for you."

She wondered if being needed also meant she was indispensable,
essential, vital, crucial...all those things she wanted to become to
him.

"Now I have you just where I want you, Regan. In my bed."

And whether he knew it or not, she had him just where she
wanted him, too. Standing in front of her and stripping, for starters.
As she watched, his hands went to the front of his jeans.

"And I have you doing what I've always fantasized about, Garth.
Taking your clothes off in front of me so I can see you naked."

She could tell from the look on his face that her words surprised
him. "You used to fantasize about me?"

"All the time. You always looked sexy in your business suits, but my imagination gets a little more risqué than that."

He shook his head. "I never knew."

"What? That I wanted you as much as you wanted me? I told you that in the kitchen earlier."

"I assumed that desire began since you've been here with me."

Boy, was he wrong. "No, it goes back further than that."

It was important that he knew everything. Not only that the desire was mutual but also that it hadn't just begun. If he understood that then it would be easier for her to build the kind of relationship they needed, regardless of whether he thought they needed it or not.

"I never knew," he said, looking a little confused. "You never said anything."

"I wasn't supposed to. You are my boss and I am a professional."

He nodded because she knew he couldn't refute that. "How long have you felt that way?"

There was no way she would tell him that she'd had a crush on him since she was sixteen, or that he was the reason she had returned to Fairbanks after her first year in college. She had heard he was back home from the military with a broken heart, and she'd been determined to fix it. Things didn't work out quite that way. He was deep in mourning for the woman he'd lost and had built a solid wall around himself, one that even his family hadn't been able to penetrate for a long while.

"The length of time doesn't matter, Garth. All you need to know is that the desire between us is mutual. Now, are you going to finish undressing or what?"

Don't miss what happens next in...
The Wife He Needs
by Brenda Jackson, the first book in her
Westmoreland Legacy: The Outlaws series!

Available November 2020 wherever
Harlequin Desire books and ebooks are sold.

Harlequin.com

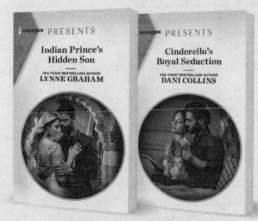

Love Harlequin romance?

DISCOVER.

Be the first to find out about promotions,
news and exclusive content!

Facebook.com/HarlequinBooks

Twitter.com/HarlequinBooks

Instagram.com/HarlequinBooks

Pinterest.com/HarlequinBooks

ReaderService.com

EXPLORE.

Sign up for the Harlequin e-newsletter and
download a free book from any series at
TryHarlequin.com

CONNECT.

Join our Harlequin community to
share your thoughts and connect
with other romance readers!
Facebook.com/groups/HarlequinConnection

HSOCIAL2020